Under
The
Sun

Under
The
Sun

JASON M. FREEMAN

iUniverse

UNDER THE SUN

iUniverse books may be ordered through booksellers or by contacting:

iUniverse
1663 Liberty Drive
Bloomington, IN 47403
www.iuniverse.com
844-349-9409

ISBN: 978-1-6632-0187-4 (sc)
ISBN: 978-1-6632-0188-1 (e)

Library of Congress Control Number: 2021900500

Print information available on the last page.

iUniverse rev. date: 01/11/2021

Preface

The best day of my life was saying hello to my son; the worst was saying goodbye. Life isn't handed to you on a platter; there are no instructions written on the walls and as hard as we try to understand, sometimes we never do. A lot of times people take so many things for granted and never see the forest for the trees.

Chapter 1

The worst day of my life started as cliche as possible in that it couldn't have been more normal.

May 24th was a gorgeous, cloudless day two weeks after Peyton's seventh birthday. It was Friday so I had to be at work early, and my wife Carrie took my son Peyton to school. Although stuck inside on such a beautiful day, I was chipper as could be, excited for the big camping trip Peyton and I had planned for tonight.

It was just before closing up and I was trying to finish up when my secretary informed me I had a phone call. I walked back into my office and picked up the phone, resting it against my shoulder. "This is Jeff."

"Hey Jeffrey, what's up?" a familiar voice asked as soon as I picked up. I shuddered internally at the greeting; Bryce knows I hate it when he calls me Jeffrey. I had a younger brother named Bryce, my rock, my best friend, my confidant. Bryce was a tall drink of water, not sure where he got it from nobody else was tall in our family. He stood at six foot two and a hundred a eighty pounds

He was in an accident when he was young and it busted his teeth up which caused his adult teeth to grow in terribly wrong. He had surgeries and all the braces and stuff but it nevertheless caused a gap in his front two teeth, turned out to be his signature. Us two were peas in a pod never really fought and were always by each other's side. He was the best man at my wedding and threw me my bachelor party. My father, when I was a young man, took Bryce and I camping to a secluded spot he called The Cover. It was a nice, flat spot of land that was perfectly surrounded by overhanging trees that kept the spot shaded. It was just a little hike up the mountain, and it was completely free and more importantly uninhabited. Another short hike up the mountain from The Cover was a nice sized pond that was creek fed. It had bass galore in that pond and we took advantage of it. Very often keeping one or two and having a fresh fish fry that night. And even another short climb from the pond was a small creek that formed a waterfall. It wasn't big at all, but the waterfall was magical. We used to sit and watch the sun fall behind the mountains with the waterfall in the foreground and it was like watching God work right in front of you.

"Just busy buddy, trying to get out of here so I can get home and load up." I said as I shuffled papers around and crammed things into my desk drawers.

"You haven't packed yet?' Bryce asked.

"You know me, man, I've gotta go over things twice and make sure we have everything."

My brother laughed. "I'll never understand why you wait until the last minute to do all that. And you know you're still gonna forget something."

"Well that's where Peyton comes in, he's home right now covering my butt."

"Well that's true. Hey listen, Jeff, I'm not going to be able to make it tonight."

"Really?"

"No man, gotta go tend to a job out near Spokane, but if I play my cards right I'll be back tomorrow afternoon and still have that night with you guys. Besides, I owe Peyton a whooping on Bass for Bass; he hammered me last time, by like seven fish."

Bass to Bass was a contest we have among us to see who caught the most fish. The winner only got bragging rights, but it was fun nevertheless.

"Yeah I haven't beaten him in a year," I laughed. "Well Bryce that sucks man, but we will hang in there tonight. I"ll see when you get there buddy."

"Y'all be careful tonight," Bryce warned. "They're calling for storms tonight."

"We will, my man. I gotta get going so I'll see you tomorrow." I hung up and went back to closing up the office for the weekend.

Peyton was in the middle of going over the camping checklist when I pulled up. "Hey monkey man, making a list and checking it twice?" I asked, pulling off my tie as I walked into the house.

I kissed his forehead as I passed, smirking when he replied, "very funny dad, a Santa Claus reference now?"

"What can I say Peyton, I'm non-seasonal."

He smiled and continued to check off his list as I walked inside. The air conditioning was a nice contrast to the warm weather outside. I threw my keys on the table and took off my dress shoes and belt.

"Is that you Jeff?" Carrie's voice rang out from the bedroom.

"Yeah babe," I yelled back.

"You know they're calling for thunderstorms tonight right?" Carrie said yelled as I walked into the bedroom where she was sitting on the bed. Her back was turned to me so I startled her when I spoke again.

"Yeah babe, Bryce said something about that too. I'm not worried about it though. The Cover usually doesn't get many storms and it's so well covered that we'll stay dry and protected even if it rains."

"Well just be careful, okay?" Carrie said, clearly still uncomfortable with the idea of thunderstorms that night.

I kissed her and pulled her into an embrace, promising we'd stay safe on our trip.

After changing clothes and methodically packing my stuff, I joined Peyton at the Rabbit to help him load it.

"Okay dad, we're set! You can check the list if you want, but I think this is all we need. But somehow I'm sure you will leave something behind." Peyton said with a teasing smiling.

"Watch it, buddy," I said, playfully rubbing his head as I passed. After checking over the list one more time we loaded up and were ready to head to The Cover.

While Peyton got in and buckled up, I walked over and kissed Carrie. "Love you," I whispered.

She smiled and yelled towards Peyton. "You guys be careful! And please don't out fish your dad again, I'm tired of hearing about it." I glanced over at her and she winked at me. I kissed her one last time and walked back over to the car, sliding into the driver's seat and backing down our curvy driveway while Peyton waved goodbye to his mother.

Sharp Township is a mountain town, so of course the commute to anywhere wasn't a straight shot. The Cover was at the end of Cold Hollow Road, a long, secluded road that dead ended at a small creek. The solitude of the road and the dense tree cover around it gave it quite the reputation as a perfect "Lover's Lane" and The Cover provided a great place to hang out for the locals.

Cold Hollow Road was about a mile long with houses tucked away along the mountain path, so high up they weren't visible from the road.

The entrance to The Cover was about half way down Cold Hollow, a small dirt path that was nearly invisible to the naked eye. Once you parked, you followed the dirt path up into the mountains toward our weekend haven.

"Dad?" Peyton asked as we drove to our destination

"Yes?".

"If Dorothy told Toto they're not in Kansas anymore, then what state is OZ in?"

Peyton was absolutely fascinated with the Wizard of OZ. His favorite movie by far, and it was from the beginning. Long before he could even talk well Carrie and I would put the movie on and he would sit and stare in awe of it. By the time he was 4 could quote it almost verbatim, and for Halloween he was the Tin Man or the Scarecrow, the boy adored that movie.

I laughed. "Son, OZ is a fictional place. Dorothy dreamt it."

"I understand that, but it has to be located somewhere, right? It has roads, even though they're yellow brick, and farms and a wizard and witches. It has to be somewhere right?"

I laughed again. "Buddy, I don't know what to tell you. It's a made up place, Dorothy came up with it in a dream."

"I think it's gotta be England."

"England?"

"Yeah England. They have brick roads, farms, and a Queen and King." Peyton explained, looking over at me.

"Well, that's true, but the King and Queen don't coincide with witches and wizards" I said.

"Well, I have an opinion on that. I think she relates the Queen to the Wicked Witch of the West and the Wizard as the King," he said, looking over at me again.

"Do tell, son," I replied.

"Well, let's say the King is the ruler, the one that pulls more strings in the kingdom correct?"

"Yes, but you're grounded if you tell your mother that." I said giggling.

"Deal, but you see what I'm saying, the wizard in the story is the King, he's the one giving hearts and brains and courage! But the Queen is almost like the secret ruler of the kingdom right? She's really the one that runs things and calls the shots and isn't afraid to get things done her way. So she tends to be seen as mean and wicked, hence the Wicked Witch of the West being the queen, the true ruler of the kingdom and one that everyone is afraid of. Also that would explain why the munchkins have English accents. I really think OZ is in England."

I pulled into the dirt path and turned the car off. "Son, where do you get this stuff? I like the Wizard of OZ too, but that's over analyzing it a bit don't you think?"

Peyton smiled. "Yeah but I can't help it Dad, I just think it's interesting! But that's enough about OZ for now, I'm ready to out fish you again, I mean, to go fishing!"

"Yeah, yeah, we'll see," I said, reaching over to give him a light noogie as we climbed out of the car. We gathered our gear from the back of the car and then set off on our trek up to The Cover. Our destination wasn't a far hike up the mountain; the path traveled across a bed of rocks and then seemed to jut straight up, but the grade wasn't as bad as it seemed. We followed the trail until it passed between two giant red oaks that stood as a proverbial gate to The Cover.

I stared up at the trees, the gate, that seemed to climb up endlessly. My dad once referred to them as Heaven's gate because he swore that they were so tall they touched heaven.

We found a good place to set up camp and began unpacking our gear, taking in the beauty of our surroundings. The Cover was a great place to hang out for the locals but it was also an amazing place for camping. The trees stood in an almost perfect circle which created a thick canopy that gave it its name. The ground was covered in thick, grainy sand, similar to a baseball field. The moisture and lack of sun left it soft and comfortable to walk on but not dusty enough to stir up a cloud while setting up camp.

It was truly perfect for a getaway for a weekend with the guys.

After we finished setting up the tent I cracked open a beer and began rigging up the poles for the fishing contest.

"Dad?" Peyton called out.

"Yeah buddy."

"You got the filet knife right?"

"You didn't put it your checklist?' I asked, looking up from the pole I was working on.

"Well I was bound to leave something off the list and it seems that was it," Peyton said.

"Well, my little forgetter, I just so happen to have one in my bag for cases just like this."

"Thank God," Peyton said with a smile. "Eating grilled fish without a filet knife would be difficult!"

"Well, no worries Peyton, I got one. And tonight may be a good time for you to learn how to filet a bass."

Peyton cut his eyes to me. "Dad, we've been over this, I'm too squeamish to do that."

"Well, son, it comes with the territory: to enjoy the grilled fish you crave, that fish must be caught, then filleted and then grilled. The circle of life."

Peyton cut his eyes at me again and shook his head. "Dad, I've told you, I'll eat fish, I'll catch it, but I'm not gonna kill it then cut it up. It's just like chicken; Ill eat it but there's no way in heck I'd chase one down and then kill it and skin it and cook it. It's inhumane!"

I laughed. "So you're a vegetarian that eats meat?"

"Well I wouldn't go so far as to say that, but why someone could adhere to that philosophy is beyond me." Peyton retorted.

"Adhere to that philosophy?" I repeated, looking back at him.

"Yeah it means-"

"I know what it means son," I interrupted with a smile. "But seriously where do you get this stuff? You're seven."

He looked at me slyly and said, "what can I say dad? I read a lot."

I chuckled and gathered the fishing poles. "Okay, buddy, let's get these lines in the water."

The pond wasn't visible from The Cover but it was just about thirty yards up a hill and through a slight clearing lined with thorn bushes. The pond was about three acres in circumference with no trees around; the few that had once stood near the edge of the water had since fallen in. Considering the bass loved to camp out in the shade under the fallen trees, this made for several great fishing spots. The layout of the pond meant you could walk around the whole circumference of the water and fish from anywhere.

"You're going down this time, son, I can feel it," I shouted playfully as Peyton walked over to his favorite fishing spot, casting his line between two fallen trees submerged under water.

And, of course, it was minutes later that I heard, "I don't think so dad." I looked over just as Peyton pulled a rather large bass from the pond.

I just shook my head and kept on fishing. I knew he was gonna beat me anyway, he always did.

We spent several hours reeling in bass from the pond, only stopping when the sun began to set. We packed up our gear and began making our way back to camp. On the trek back, I noticed a little cloud cover creeping up in the distance but it wasn't enough to be concerning. Still, I kept my eye on it as we walked back, listening as Peyton bragged about winning the fishing contest.

Once back at camp, Peyton began gathering up wood for the fire while I cleaned the fish for dinner.

"Dad, what do you think happens when you die?"

I was stunned at the question and looked up from the fish I was cleaning. "Well I would like to think that if we lived a good and proper life that we would get invited to heaven and spend eternity in bliss."

"Does it ever scare you?" he asked.

"No, I can't say that it does son. It's inevitable so there's nothing to be scared of."

"But do you ever think that maybe it's not what you imagine, that maybe it's awful when you die?"

Again, I was stunned by the question and thought for a second to give him a decent answer. "No," I said eventually. "For two reasons: one, a thought like that would drive a person like me crazy, and two, you've seen the sunsets and sunrises here at The Cover. When something that beautiful exists, then there's gotta be a heaven. Life is too peculiar and too beautiful for there not to be something out there! And where are you getting this Peyton? Why are you asking me this?"

He just laughed and shook his head. "Just curious what you thought. I know there's something out there, but just wanted to hear your view."

"You are seriously too smart for your own good, son!" I said, ruffling his hair lightly before going back to cleaning the fish. I lit the fire, stoking the flames until they were ready, and then slapped the fish filets on the frying pan nestled just above the flames.

We sat quietly as we ate and watched as the setting sun was replaced with the clouds rolling in. It started to drizzle around

10:00pm so we decided to call it a night and head for the tent. The rain would put the fire out so we tucked away the rest of our gear and got ready to turn in.

As we laid down in our sleeping bags, Peyton said, "I miss Bryce, I wish he was here tonight."

"I know buddy, but he said he would be here tomorrow," I replied.

"Yeah but I wanted to beat y'all in the fish off two nights in a row. It loses a little luster just beating *you* two times in a row." Peyton taunted.

I just shook my head and said goodnight.

He grinned and said, "goodnight, you're my hero daddy!"

I smiled and we both drifted off to sleep.

It was around 1:00 am when I first heard the wind slicing through the trees. Heavy rain was pelting the tent and lightning flashed in the distance, a deep crack of thunder echoing over The Cover a few seconds later. At first I didn't think much of it, we've been through plenty of storms over the years. But then an awful sound, the sound of cracking trees and splintering wood, cut through the air over the pounding of rain. A strong wind gusted through The Cover, breaking branches and knocking smaller trees over all around us.

My heart was racing as I woke Peyton up. "Get up buddy, there's a really bad storm out there and we need to be awake till it blows over!"

He rubbed his eyes and sat up and looked up at the tent that was lit up with the brightness of the lightning that surrounded us. The wind was howling in the woods and the storm increased.

We huddled together nervously, the cracking of the trees getting worse and the rumbling thunder sounding like two trains colliding.

Just then the tent split at the top and rain poured in on top of us.

We both jumped and I told Peyton to stay still as I unzipped the tent and reached up to try and grab the ripped fabric and secure it. The wind kept howling and the rain stung against my face as it continued to pelt our tent.

I frantically grasped for something to try and keep the tent secure but there was nothing inside the tent to repair the rip and keep it grounded. I remembered I had a rope next to the cooler, so I braved the storm and stepped outside to get it.

No sooner had I exited the tent did the loudest noise I had ever heard erupted all around me. At the same time a blinding light consumed me and I was lifted and thrown about fifteen feet.

When I came to everything was silent and my whole body hurt. I sat up, disoriented and very groggy. I was soaking wet and bleeding from a wound in my forehead. I gathered myself and stood up shakily to get my bearings.

Everything was so calm and quiet and it took a minute to realize something was wrong with the quiet silence. The panic hit.

I ran to the storm-ravaged tent, desperately screaming for Peyton with no answer.

My heart was pounding in my chest as I found the flashlight from the tent and beat it against the palm of my hand to get it to turn on. Still screaming for Peyton, I got the light to come on and went searching for my son. Staggering through the battered trees, about 20 feet to my right, I saw the worst thing I could have ever imagined.

Peyton's limp, bloody body laying face down by a tree. I ran to him and dropped to my knees, pulling his cold, wet body into my arms.

"Peyton, talk to me buddy," I begged with quivering lips. I lifted him higher in my arms and saw the extent of his injuries and knew it was too late. The lightning strike that had thrown me away from the tent had thrown him back as well, his small body colliding with a tree.

I wailed into the blackness that surrounded me.

Hugging his lifeless body to my chest, I collapsed back into the mud. The pain was overwhelming and I screamed at the emptiness that filled me.

Chapter 2

I met my son for the first time the way most fathers do: after a sleepless night following a mad dash to the hospital. It was hard to believe that just a few hours before I'd been deep asleep and dreaming and was suddenly awoken by my wife's heavy breathing.

There were three deep breaths and then a wince of pain and then Carrie was screaming at me to "get my butt up, it's time!" Yes she was in labor and I immediately went from dreaming to frantically looking for things that I didn't think I would need for this venture.

I had packed meticulously for when she went into labor and now all I could do was search for things that I just now realized we may need, like our toothpaste and socks.

I listened as Carrie did her breathing exercises and cursed me every way from Sunday. I finally found the toothpaste and took a second to stop and take a look in the mirror. The bags under my eyes had already started to form and my beard stubble was in full affect. I splashed some water on my face and swished some around in my mouth. When I looked back at the mirror I smiled; I was about to become a father.

Some men panic and some are elated. I was the latter, I couldn't wait to be a dad!

I walked out the bathroom door and glanced at the bedside alarm clock, noticing it was 2:39 in the morning. Carrie had already walked out to the car but I could still hear her cursing me as she headed out the front door.

I did one more quick sweep of the house and then scurried to the door behind my expecting wife. We got into the car and I put the pedal to the metal.

"Don't you wreck us before we even get to the hospital, Jeff," Carrie warned as the tires squealed on our way out of the driveway. I always thought that was cliche: don't get us in a wreck on the way to the hospital. I had no intention of wrecking but then I suppose no one does when they're driving. And if wrecks happen so often on the way to hospital in this scenario then why don't more couples spring for an ambulance?

These thoughts were running through my mind as I raced down the winding mountain hills of Sharp Township. I held Carrie's hand as we made our way to the hospital. Neither of us talked, whether through nerves or excitement, I'm not sure, but we spoke not a word until I pulled up to the emergency room.

I hopped out and was busy helping Carrie out of the car when a man noticed us and brought over a wheelchair. She plopped down with a wince and the man wheeled her into the hospital while I parked the car.

I grabbed all the bags and anything else I could in one trip; I didn't want to have to go back and get anything else if it could be avoided. Now here's the most interesting part of all this, a part not largely covered in the books you read and the classes you take. After all the panic and adrenaline of getting to the hospital fades and you're sure your wife is in good hands, there's nothing left to do but wait.

And there's a lot of waiting.

I never expected that nor was I ever told that this may happen.

Carrie and I were put into a room no bigger than our bedroom at home. It smelled of clean sheets and Lysol and had a TV in the corner that was so tiny you needed a telescope to see the numbers on a jersey if you watched sports on it.

After a while a doctor came in to examine Carrie and get her hooked up to an IV. He told us to relax, that he'd be back to check on us later and then we.... well we waited again.

"Are you comfortable sweetie? Thirsty or hungry? Anything I can do?" I asked after the doctor shut the door behind him.

"No Jeff, even if I were hungry or thirsty I couldn't eat or drink anything with all this," she said, gesturing to the IV in her arm.

I smiled and nodded; it occurred to me that ice chips was all she could eat and the IV was for her fluids. What can I say, I wasn't very astute on all this birth stuff.

The next few hours were long and drawn out with nurses and doctors periodically coming in and out. I tried watching the TV in the corner but it was so small I couldn't focus on it.

At some point Carrie fell asleep so I turned off the television and went for a walk. I found a water fountain in the hall and then walked outside to get a breath of fresh Washington air.

It was early May and the air was crisp and cold but not bitterly cold; it felt great in my lungs this morning. I walked back in and stumbled upon the glass wall with the newborns on the other side.

I stopped and stared for a minute and my heart filled with joy knowing soon I would be staring through this glass at my own son! I walked back to our room with a smile only to walk in a room full of people and my wife screaming to every ounce of her soul "where the hell have you been!"

It was time, soon I would get to meet Peyton!

Chapter 3

Ok So I've given you a lot so far, so let me get to the introductions.

I'm Jeff Lockler I'm a 29 year old banker from a small town called Sharp-Township, Washington. Standing about five foot seven and a hundred and forty lbs. I was a proud bald headed man, out of choice too.

I was raised in a Christian household to two wonderful parents, Glenn and Joyce Lockler.

Our parents were tragically killed in a car accident October 24th 1971, my senior year of college and the same year I met my wife. It hit Bryce very hard and with him being three years younger than me he was in a bit more tougher spot. Thank god that they had left the house to me and a little money to Bryce so I was able to give it to him and luckily the house was paid off in full so Bryce was able to take the money and start a carpentry business.

As for me I was majoring in economics with a minor in business and since I was able to stay in college and graduate, banking seemed like a simple and easy path out of college.

I, being from Washington, attended the glorious University of Washington in Seattle, go Huskies! I grew up a Husky fan, my dad was a huge fan and I actually followed in his footsteps by attending and majoring in economics.

I quickly rushed through the door and to her side and of course said "I'm so sorry honey, I went for a breath of fresh air and then-"

Carrie quickly interrupted with a vengeance, "SHUT UP JEFF! I'M HAVING A BABY SO SAVE YOUR MONOLOGUE FOR LATER!"

I obliged and shut my mouth quickly and came up to the head of the bed to comfort her through the intense labor.

After a few hours my back started to hurt and sweat started dripping into my eyes. The buzzing from the fluorescent lights overhead was also causing a headache of epic proportion. But I stayed silent and fought through it; Carrie was doing all the work and dealing with the pain of delivering our son.

The mid-wife suddenly looked over at me and grinned and said "I see a full head of hair, would you like to see and feel?"

So I was all about seeing, but the feel got me a bit. I let go of Carrie's leg for a minute and looked over and did see a head of hair, but I was still iffy on the feeling of it part. But I manned up and reached down and rubbed my soon to be son's full blown head of hair, I swear we could've combed it.

"Carrie" I whispered "Peyton doesn't just have hair already he's got enough for you to style right now!" I tried to edge in a little light comedy but she was non the more amused, as she kept on in agonizing pain to get Peyton out.

After what seemed like another six hours, which were somewhat of a blur, I hear the words Carrie and I had longed for this whole time "he's here!"

Peyton was born at 2:56 pm. with a head full of hair and the most precious green eyes.

"Oh my gosh he's so tiny," Carrie whimpered as she draped her arms around me pulling me to her. I pressed my face against hers, the sweat poured from her brow and she trembled with exhaustion.

We watched in awe as they carried Peyton over to be weighed and measured. After a few minutes, they bundled Peyton up and brought him over and laid him on Carrie's chest where she couldn't control the tears as she stared into his gorgeous green eyes.

I looked at both of them and my heart skipped a beat. I then looked at just Carrie; her beauty was nothing short of angelic and with all this going on I could only think of one thing, and that was the first time I met her.

Chapter 4

Carrie was born Carrie Freeman in Eugene, Oregon a short 29 years before this glorious day.

A short, yet tall with personality was Carrie. A gorgeous, long haired brunette, freckled faced girl that had a smile that could only be described as heavenly.

Her parents raised her as devoted a catholic as there could be. Three times a week in church, tithing, mission trips, and everything in between. She left the college town of Eugene to another college town to attend the University of Washington. Which is where she met me in a fortuitous meeting at a football game.

My buddies and I were tailgating in the frigid Novembers that Washington brought. UCLA was in town and this game was huge, because we were undefeated with only Washington State to go. Well as we were tailgating we noticed a group of women next to us who were cooking hamburgers on a small grill. One of my friends dared me to walk over and very politely ask for a hamburger.

Well it just so happened that I was hungry, and had enough beers in me that I was feeling a little more courageous than normal. The only problem was there were only four burgers and four ladies so naturally I didn't feel right taking someone's lunch. So I said thanks and walked back food less and a little embarrassed.

Moments later I heard the softest voice ever and when I turned it was Carrie and she offered me half her hamburger. We spent the rest of the day together and after the game we walked about campus just talking. I remember getting to her dorm room and kissing her cheek.

She said "You've got to be kidding me?"

I was shocked "what, what's the matter?" I asked.

"All day we have spent together, all day talking and me touching your hand and laughing at your silly jokes, and a kiss on the cheek is all I'm going to get?"

She seemed pissed so I smiled and in all my gentlemanly way I could muster I planted a passionate kiss on her and we fell into the door and almost fell into the floor. We finished the kiss and I had to help her up.

I asked "was that good enough for you?" And she smiled and shrugged her shoulders and replied "It will do for now."

She opened the door and went inside. I fell against the wall and slid down putting my face into my hands. Needless to say we haven't spent a day apart since then. She grounded me in a way, no not like I was in trouble and was forced to sleep on the couch and be back home by a certain time.

No she kept me in a spot to where I didn't stray to far from the normal. She made sense to me, and I made sense to her. Then love of course took over and cupid's arrow took aim and we were one. We married one glorious day on seventh of July, in a ceremony at her church.

We had the reception at Bryce's house and he had built this heavenly arch that he had us walk through.

I asked Bryce "dude why the arch?" He replied "well in Catholicism they have what is called a Plenary Indulgence, which in lamen's terms is a proverbial door that once you have passed through your sins are forgiven. So with Carrie being Catholic I thought it would be cool"

I truly didn't know what to say except "wow man, just when I thought you couldn't get any smarter" I hugged him and kissed his check. Now getting back to the best day of my life!

Peyton Allen Lockler came into the world that day and made my life complete. That warm, tiny green-eyed beauty I held that day couldn't have made me prouder to be alive. Looking down at my newborn son, I've never felt such love and excitement. Who knew something so small and innocent could produce such a strong emotion from a grown man.

Carrie and I stayed in the hospital for a few more days while she breastfed and tried to sleep as best as she could. I helped as best I could and tried to sleep but it was nearly impossible with nurses and doctors constantly coming in and out. I couldn't wait to get home and neither could Carrie.

When the day finally came where we could take our baby boy home, both Carrie and Peyton were wheeled to the entrance of the hospital while I went to retrieve the car. Excitement and the nerves of a brand new parent meant it took a few minutes to figure out all the straps and buckles of the car seat but eventually Peyton was strapped in and ready to go home. Carrie slid into the passenger seat and I got in behind the wheel and our little family was ready to go.

Neither of us spoke during the drive, possibly from anticipation, but the brisk, twenty minute drive felt like it only took a minute. We got back to the house and I helped Carrie out and then hustled to grab Peyton and the bags and then make our way inside.

I laid Peyton down in the crib in his room and just watched him. I was so overwhelmed with the idea of having a child and starting this new life as a parent that I couldn't stop the happy tears that streamed down my face.

Carrie and I bought our dream house two years before Peyton came along. It was a two story house with a screened in back porch that overlooked the small town below. We had his room set up in the far corner of the house, a cozy little nook with a large bay window and a great view looking over Sharp-Township.

We stayed in Sharp-Township because my bank was close by and the church she liked was also very close. Sharp Township was a little quiet community, based on logging mostly. The town had started to grow a bit recently, the logging attracting lumberjacks and businessmen abroad. Sharp Township lay in the foothills of the Cascade Range of mountains and on a clear day you could look out and see Mount Rainier.

Peyton was an easy child for the most part. He struggled sleeping through the night for six months or so but I've heard of worse stories so we counted our blessings. Time flew by and before we knew it he was starting kindergarten and playing tee-ball.

Life was almost perfect for us three, and more like a hit TV. Show. Carrie was volunteering at the church routinely, and I was forever teaching Peyton the ways of the woods. We camped and fished and spent every moment we could at The Cover, sometimes a little more than Carrie would like, but she understood it was our thing.

He was a very smart kid; sometimes I worried he was too smart. He was in advanced classes in school and had a wit that always astonished me. We had quite a relationship, him and me.

Every night as Carrie and I put him to bed, he would kiss us both and say "you're my angel mamma and you're my hero daddy."

How could that not melt your heart? We lived as normally as we could; we squabbled occasionally and sometimes we had to punish Peyton, but lived as gracefully as we could.

And for a while that was enough.

Chapter 5

I remember waking up in a hospital bed, my whole body aching with the taste of what could only be described as blood and dirt lingering in my mouth. Everything felt blurry and hazy, almost like a dream. But I could still hear the way the rain pelted against the tent in my head and that awful crash of thunder.

The memory hit me all at once and I sat straight up and screamed, "Peyton!"

I looked at the shocked faces of my friends and family surrounding me. "Where's Peyton?" I asked shakily. I knew in my heart what happened but couldn't bring myself to accept it.

"Where's Peyton?" I screamed again.

At that moment I saw Carrie across the room and the pain and anguish in her eyes was enough to floor me. I felt myself sob, anger and misery filling me.

Bryce entered the room and we locked eyes. He fell to his knees at my bedside and clutched me to him. "It's impossible to say how sorry I am, Jeff. God, I'm so sorry."

The sobs became louder in the room and the fluorescent light seemed to fade into black. I seemed to go into a trance and didn't remember much after that.

Carrie never spoke, she sat somberly in the chair as a very unfortunate doctor was given the unenviable task of telling us how our son died. The lightning strike was more than enough to kill a small child like Peyton but it had been the force of the explosion that had led to his death; he broke his neck when he crashed into the tree.

Carrie vomited as he spoke, overwhelmed by the horror of our son's death. Eventually the doctor left the room and I moved to sit down next to Carrie, wrapping my arm around her shoulders.

"Come on guys, let's get you home," Bryce said after a few minutes. It only took a few minutes to gather our stuff but it felt like a lifetime. The ride home was silent; I sat staring out one window and Carrie laid her head in my lap and cried.

The lights of the buildings blurred by as Bryce drove us home. I absently rubbed Carrie's sweaty forehead and felt her tears soaking through the leg of my pants.

When we finally got home, Bryce and I helped Carrie inside. She was exhausted from grief and lack of sleep and it took both of us to move her into the bedroom. Once there, we laid her down in our bed and she curled up on her side and stared at the wall blankly.

I shut the door behind and walked to the kitchen where Bryce was sitting. I made my way over to the refrigerator and searched for anything with alcohol in it. Finding a beer, I opened it and downed it within seconds.

I threw the empty beer bottle away and grabbed another one. "Bryce I've never seen anything like it!" I said, slightly out of breath from downing the first beer. "The sound was so loud, deafening in fact. I'll never get that sound out of my head Bryce." I shook my head and opened the second beer, taking another long drink. "The crazy thing is that it seems like it was meant to be."

"Meant to be?" Bryce asked.

I finished the second beer and went back for a third. "It was like that storm was out for us. It was relentless Bryce, it feels like it came after us."

"Jeff, I know it may feel like that but you know that's silly. It was just a storm, an extra strong storm-"

"Exactly! A storm that strong hasn't hit The Cover in over thirty years and I couldn't even protect my son from it!" I screamed, starting to feel the effects of the alcohol and the crushing grief that was threatening to overwhelm me. "I couldn't protect my son from the weather, Bryce, from the damn weather!"

I slumped down against the refrigerator and Bryce knelt down next to me, putting his arms around my shoulders. He was crying too. "Jeff, I know for an absolute fact that you did everything to protect Peyton. You did all you could!"

I looked up at him through my tears and shook my head. "I'm not so sure I did."

I pushed myself up off the floor and slowly made my way to the couch. The beer in my hand sloshed as I collapsed onto the couch, curling into the cushions drunkenly. Bryce sat down next to me and rubbed my back. "Jeff," he began, trying to comfort me in some way. "I have no idea the sorrow and misery you're feeling right now. But I do know that you have to be strong for Carrie, and for Peyton. You know he would want you to be strong. You know I will always be here for you. I will never turn my back and if there's anything you need please don't hesitate to ask," he said, hugging me again and crying softly.

I reached up and hugged him too and soon drifted off to sleep.

I woke up the next morning with a massive headache and bolted off the couch to make it to the bathroom before I threw up. I wasn't sure if it was from the alcohol or from grief but it didn't matter. I stood up and washed my face with cold water in an effort to wake myself up. I looked at myself in the mirror and saw the scars.

The physical scars stood out yes, but the mental scars stood out even more. I couldn't stand to look at myself anymore and left the bathroom. I walked down the hallway and looked in on Carrie.

"Carrie honey, you okay?" She looked at me blankly and nodded and then rolled back over in a fetal position. She was wrapped in a duvet and had tissues laying all over the bed.

I left our room and turned to walk towards Peyton's room and after one step I fell to my knees. I screamed and it turned into a sob. "Peyton, oh God!"

Seeing his room was too much. I lay on my back and stared up at the ceiling. Tears stung my eyes but I couldn't stop them. I laid there and wept in front of my son's room, now silent and empty.

Eventually I pulled myself up off the floor and stood up, shielding my eyes so I didn't have to look into my son's empty room again. I shuffled back down the hallway to check on Carrie but she was still in the same position; she hadn't moved at all during my outburst.

I walked to the kitchen and stood for a few minutes, dizzy and incoherent. I could barely breathe and the weight and magnitude of my grief threatened to topple me. I reached into the fridge and grabbed another beer, finishing it in about three swallows. Finding no more beer in the fridge, I found a bottle of chardonnay and poured a glass and went and sat on the couch.

I just sat there and stared at the wall. I didn't have the energy to turn on the tv on, or the radio, or anything. My mind bounced between racing and going completely blank I truly couldn't hold a thought. I could hear the air conditioning kick on and off and the sunlight seemed to trickle in and out of the shades.

The flickering sunlight started to drive me crazy so I got up and closed every shade in the house and turned off every light. I finished the glass of wine while I was up and went back and grabbed the bottle.

I found a blanket on the recliner and wrapped myself, stretching back on the couch and guzzling the bottle of wine. It tasted awful but I didn't care, it seemed to numb the pain and fill the hole that was now prominent in my life. The blanket smelled like Peyton and I held it to my face, breathing in his scent with tears streaming down my face.

I began to feel sick to my stomach and the room was spinning a little at this point so I closed my eyes and once again passed out.

I don't remember much of the next year to be perfectly honest.

My daily routine consisted of an unbroken cycle of drinking and mourning. Each day I managed to get up and go to work and then stumble back home, pick up a bottle of anything alcoholic, and drink myself to sleep in front of the TV in the living room.

I lost 42 pounds after Peyton died and barely spoke to anyone except Carrie and Bryce. I do remember Peyton's funeral though; nothing could make me forget that, no amount of anything.

Carrie fainted when she saw the casket; I can't say I blamed her. As much as I wanted to help her, I couldn't; I was too lost in my own grief to focus on anything else. Bryce stood by her the whole time, his arm wrapped around her shoulders as she sobbed. He squeezed my hand as we made our way to the cemetery.

Peyton's service was beautiful and it helped to have our friends and family there to support us. The car ride home was awful, much worse than the ride home after it happened. It was less surreal after the funeral, it seemed more final, and I hated it.

I don't remember a whole lot after that until five months later we went to visit his grave for the first time. I remember staring at his headstone, trying to understand the words on the cold, grey stone, but my brain refused to accept that they were about Peyton. My smart, bright, wonderful son was reduced to a few lines on a headstone and I couldn't accept it. We didn't visit again for a long time after that, it was just too hard.

Carrie went back to work after about two months but she never could bring herself to volunteer with the church or do anything else she used to enjoy. We both seemed to just be walking through life in a daze. We never did anything together anymore, hell, we barely spoke to each other. Each day we'd get home, eat dinner, and then disappear into our own individual bubbles.

Carrie fell into the bottle just like I did. Every night before bed she would pour a glass wine and stand in front Peyton's room and just stare. She tried several times to get me to do it but I refused. I couldn't look at his room and I couldn't bare to go in it.

I asked her one night why she did that to herself and she looked at me with tears in her eyes and said, "I can imagine him sitting in there like this."

She was a stronger person than I was, I guess. The loss of our son had taken a toll on our marriage. We barely spoke to each other, let alone be intimate. Even on our anniversary the only thing we could manage to do was hold each other and cry silently in our bedroom.

Other than that one night, we didn't even sleep in the same bed together. I slept on the couch and had made the living room into a makeshift bedroom. Our lives had changed forever but I did feel like it was my fault we had grown apart the way we did.

Another year passed, nothing much had changed at all. That's when Carrie woke me up on a Saturday morning.

"Jeff, Jeff wake up" she said, shaking me.

I opened one eye and slurred, "what, Carrie?"

"Jeff, we have to talk."

I sat up and reached for the bottle of bourbon sitting on the coffee table. After a couple of swigs and a loud clearing of my throat I looked at Carrie.

"What about?"

"We can't live like this anymore, Jeff." Carrie said softly.

"Live like what?" I said swigging my bourbon again.

"Like this Jeff, the drinking, the misery. We're destroying ourselves. It feels like we're not even married anymore. We don't make love, we don't sleep in the same bed, hell we don't even talk to each other. We come home, eat dinner, if that, and both go our separate ways, which both end up at the bottom of a bottle somehow!"

She was staring at me intently and all I could think to say was "Well, I thought you wanted the same thing too?"

She stood up and paced as she said "I didn't know what I wanted, or if I would ever want anything again after Peyton died! But I was laying in bed last night and got up to get some wine, and it hit me."

"What hit you?" I asked.

"That we can't live like this anymore, Jeff! Peyton wouldn't want this for us, he wouldn't want us to stop living our lives completely. I've thought long and hard about it Jeff and I'm not just gonna give up life. We still have our whole lives-."

I shook my head and stood up. "And so did Peyton, Carrie! Don't talk to me about all the years ahead of me when our son died before he ever got to experience his own life. Life is fragile, and frail, and can be gone in a flash, so don't bark up that tree."

I snatched the bottle up off the table again and took a long drink.

"Jeff, Peyton's death was an accident. I know it's painful but God works in mysterious ways-"

"Oh God works in mysterious ways?" I interrupted angrily. "You're damn right he works in mysterious ways! How about crazy fucked up ways that took our seven year old son from us? That's as mysterious as you get Carrie, and what the hell could he possibly have gotten from it? Oh I know, because he was the best person on this planet. He was our son, Carrie, not his, ours, and he took him from us. That doesn't sound mysterious, that sounds selfish!"

I screamed in frustration and kicked the door open to the garage, stalking inside and sitting down in the corner to regain my composure. After a few minutes I calmed down and went back inside. I looked around for Carrie but didn't see her, so I walked to the bedroom and saw her sitting on the edge of the bed.

"Carrie, I'm sorry. But things aren't ever gonna be the same. You and I may never be able to get back to our normal selves. If it's something you think you can do then great, but I'm not sure it's something I can do."

She wiped her eyes and turned to look at me, "What are you saying?" she asked.

"I don't think I will ever live a normal life again."

"Why?" she asked.

"Because it was my fault Carrie! I was out there, I took him out there, and I couldn't stop it!"

"Jeff it was an accident, nobody could've stopped it." Carrie said apathetically.

"No, you don't understand Carrie, it's like it was coming for us. I should've stayed there with him and maybe I could've broken his fall or taken the brunt of the impact. I couldn't save him that night and I'll never forgive myself for that. If I go back to pretending nothing happened it would be like forgiving me, and I can't be forgiven!"

31

"Oh Jeff, honey, it's not your fault, it's not your fault at all. We can get through this together. You can't just toss the rest of your life aside because you feel guilty about this! God…"

"Will you please quit with the God crap?" I demanded angrily. "What kind of God do you want to worship? The one who kills innocent little boys? Because no way will I worship the one you keep referring to!"

I grabbed my coat from the coat rack and started walking towards the door, snatching my keys from the hook next to the door "Things will never be the same Carrie."

I slammed the door and buttoned my coat, ignoring the sound of Carrie sobbing through the door. I got in my car and took off down the road, heading for nowhere. Eventually, like so many days before, I found myself pulling into the parking lot of a nearby liquor store.

I looked in the rear view mirror as I parked and felt a wave of nausea sweep through me. A disheveled, broken man leered back at me from the mirror. I was unshaven, I had a cold sore in the left corner of my mouth, and I looked like I hadn't slept in a year.

I looked out at the people staring at me as I sat in the car, not truly knowing what I was doing. I didn't want the alcohol, not really, yet I knew I was going to buy some and drink it until I either slept or needed more. That had become my life, it was the only thing that seemed normal.

Reluctantly, I opened the door and headed into the store. I had a coat on, the brown fabric reeking of alcohol and mildew, and flip flops. It was a beautiful day outside, the sun shining and birds chirping, but I could barely see.

I looked like a hobo staggering into the store. I opened the door hard and it swung back on me almost knocking me over. I made my way through the store back to where my favorite bourbon was kept. I grabbed a bottle and walked up to the counter. I sat the bottle down and reached for my wallet, only then noticing that it was damp with sweat. It was hot outside but I was wearing a jacket.

The clerk was giving me a nasty look so I gave one right back. "I guess your life is peaches and cream huh?" I said snidely.

He made a face when I said that but said nothing as I shoved a few crumpled bills across the counter and grabbed the bottle again. "Don't judge me asshole just give me my change and let me get out of here."

As soon as the clerk passed my change back to me, I snatched it up and dropped it in my pocket, turning on my heel and making my way to the door. I bumped right into another patron entering the store but didn't slow down to see if she had fallen or not.

I got in the car, twisted the cap off the bourbon, and took a deep gulp. The liquor store and the parking lot disappeared behind me as I drove off, no real destination in mind. I wasn't sure what I was angry about but I honked at people who weren't going fast enough and screamed and punched the steering wheel. I rode right up on people, daring them to hit the brakes.

I drove aimlessly for a long time before it ever dawned on me where I was going. It hadn't even occurred to me that I stopped my car in front of a large patch of trees with a little dirt path snaking off into the woods. I sat there, staring at the woods in front of me, and found myself getting out of the car.

I stumbled as I walked, tripping over tree roots and loose rocks and I worked my way up a hill. I was out of breath and my heart was racing, and I was clueless at why I was doing this all. I took a step and lost my footing which sent me sprawling down the hill into a thorn patch, spilling my bourbon all over me.

I was exhausted, drunk, and very confused, but I got up and dusted myself off and kept going, not knowing what lay ahead. I finally came to a clearing at the top of the hill and sat down on the ground. Bleeding and panting to catch my breath, I let out a frustrated scream. It hadn't occurred to me until just then, I was sitting in The Cover.

Drunk and struggling to breathe from my fall, I looked up at the trees surrounding me and felt nauseous.

The Cover looked just as it did two years ago, gorgeous, tall red oak trees that swayed in the breeze that stirred through their branches. The green, lush leaves dropped and floated in the air like small balloons, and played gracefully with the wind.

I stumbled around for a few minutes, gasping for breath and grabbing at my side where I bruised a rib when I fell. I dropped to my knees and slumped over boneless when I got to where Peyton had been killed.

There was nothing there, just nature, yet I frantically looked for something to show what had happened. Blood, an indention, anything at all that could be symbolic. Of course there was nothing, but I searched on my hands and knees for anything at all. I just had to have something, anything for peace of mind.

Which was stupid because there was no peace of mind, no normalcy any longer. Peyton was our life, he was our pride and joy and was taken away far too young.

How do you recover from something like that?

Maybe Carrie was right, maybe we had to find a way to deal with our grief and learn to move on. She hadn't forgotten about Peyton but she was learning to live without him, to move into the "after" of before and after Peyton's death. She was moving forward but I wasn't, I couldn't.

I lay flat on my back and I wailed as I looked up at the leaves floating down above me. I lay there exactly like I did that awful night two years ago. But the hole inside me felt like it was filling somehow, I just didn't know how to describe it.

And that's when I heard it,

"Dad."

I sat up and looked around, not sure if my mind was playing tricks on me or not. The voice sounded like it came from above me, above the trees, and it sounded exactly like Peyton's voice.

I stood up, dusting myself off and flicking ants off my arm. "Hello?" I called out, listening as my voice traveled through the trees.

"Hello, is someone there?" I yelled out again. I walked around in a circle, just looking through the forest.

Then it came again, "Dad, November 17th."

I spun around, startled, looking in every direction for someone. It was definitely a voice, Peytons's voice, but there was nobody there.

I kept yelling, hoping it was someone messing with me. My heart was beating hard and I was sweating profusely and I was clueless as to what I should do. Should I run, should I stay and figure it out, what was I doing? I found myself absently looking around for my bottle of bourbon but quickly remembered I had spilled it when I fell.

That's when I saw it.

It was a circle of sunlight showing straight through the trees and the shade. It was amazing and I was oddly drawn to it; I walked towards it like it was pulling me there. In a zombie-like state, I made my way over to this circle of light. My heart was beating so hard that I felt it in my temples and sweat that poured over my brow stung my eyes.

This was impossible. I had been to The Cover hundreds of times and never saw sunlight creep through the leaves like this. I mean it's the reason for the name it has.

I got there and tried to look up at the light but it was so blinding and brilliant I had to look away. I took a few steps back and just stared at its beauty.

There was something unexplainable about this light, something almost angelic.

Then the voice came again. "Dad, November 17th."

I looked around again, desperately searching for him but again there was no one there.

Finally, I called out hesitantly, "Peyton?"

His voice answered back, "Dad, November 17th."

I fell backwards, landing hard on my butt, and then scrambled up and took off running, the trees blurring in my peripherals as I ran. Sharp, hard rock stabbed into the soles of my shoes and by the time I finally stopped, panting heavily to catch my breath, my feet were sore and burning.

It felt like knives were stabbing through my lungs and a sharp pinch pulled at my right side as I struggled to catch my breath. Terrified, I crouched down behind a tree and stared back at The Cover.

What the hell was going on? Was I somehow asleep and this was all a strange, vivid dream? Was I dead and didn't realize it and this was my own personal hell? Was I having an alcohol induced hallucination? All these things rushed through my mind like a freight train.

I sat down on the ground, still panting, and kept searching the trees for any sign of anyone else around me. After a few minutes, when I was able to breathe again, I told myself that I had to go back.

I didn't want to, the whole situation was terrifying, but deep down there was something about this that I had to go through.

It was beyond me that Peyton was talking to me. I wasn't sure what was happening, I wasn't sure of anything anymore.

I rose from my hiding spot, wiping the sweat from my brow, and reluctantly walked back to The Cover. The circle of light was still hovering there and I felt a lump rise in my throat as I got closer. I stopped and looked around again, hoping for the trick to be over with and my pranksters to come forward. And again there was no one there; all I could see was trees and all I could hear were the birds chirping.

Peyton's voice rang out again. "Dad, November 17th."

Anger began to replace the fear and I called out into the trees, "whoever is doing this the joke's over. It's not funny and you're gonna be lucky if I don't kick your ass!"

My voice echoed around and a few birds flew off but nobody came out of the woods and no voice called out to me. Instead, I heard my son's voice again. "Dad, November 17th."

It was definitely Peyton, it had to be.

I put my hand over my mouth and started to tremble. I could taste the dirt and sweat on my hand.

"Peyton, is that really you son?" I mustered up the courage to say. I didn't get an answer so I called out again "Peyton, please answer me!"

All I heard was the rustling of the trees, and thoughts in my head.

I know I heard Peytons voice and wanted so badly to talk to him. The anger I was feeling quickly turned to grief. This was crazy, I know it was, but I know that was his voice.

My whole body hurt; my fingernails were bleeding from gasping at the dirt and my feet were still burning from running earlier, but I wasn't leaving until I heard his voice again.

"Peyton," I began, staring off into the trees, desperately searching for some sign of him. "Son, I don't know if you can hear me but I would love for you to talk to me again. When you died, a piece of me died too. Your mother and I, we miss you son, we miss you more than life itself, and wish I could have one more second with you!"

I collapsed back to the ground and looked out through the forest that surrounded me, the gorgeous, tall trees looked taller in my world now. "Dad, November 17th." Peyton's voice said again.

That's when the circle of light evaporated into the shade of the enormous trees that loomed above me. I suddenly felt a sense of peace I hadn't experienced since Peyton died. It swept through me and suddenly I felt like I had a purpose, like I was meant to do something. I wiped the tears from my unshaven face and felt the grit from the dirt on my hands.

I took a deep breath, glanced one last time at the spot where the light had faded away, and sprinted towards my car.

I drove like a madman, weaving in and out of traffic blindly. I could hear the other cars honking behind me but the sounds of the car horns were distant and far away. The lights behind me looked like dwindling Christmas lights that faded into the night. My tires screeched with every hard turn I took and I could smell burnt rubber.

The dark, mountain road seemed endless and I was breathing so hard the windows were fogged from the inside. I was hot and sweating but didn't care. I didn't care that I could get pulled over or even if someone reported me. It didn't slow me down a bit; I had to get home and tell Carrie what happened.

I finally pulled into our driveway and noticed all the lights were off which was odd. Carrie was usually sitting on the couch drinking wine and watching reruns of old sitcoms. But the house was desolate as I hopped out of the car and ran towards the garage door. I tripped as I swung the heavy wooden door open, spilling myself onto our linoleum kitchen floor.

I jumped up and darted to the bedroom, expecting to find Carrie asleep. "Carrie, honey, wake up." I yelled as I ran down the hall.

I got no answer, so I called out again, "Carrie?" I peered into the dark, empty room and saw no movement. I flipped on the light to see the bed neatly made with brand new pillow covers placed perfectly on the duvet. I looked around the room, noticing that the bright, yellow walls made the room look much bigger and much emptier.

I looked on Carrie's night table and saw a picture of Peyton when he was just a baby. I sat on the bed and picked up the picture, hugging it to my chest tightly as if it were Peyton.

The lump settled in my throat and, I put the picture back down, standing again and walking through the house in search of Carrie. "Carrie, babe, I've got something amazing to tell you."

Still no answer.

I went for the fridge to get a drink, and I stopped and looked at the beer and wine in there. I reached twice for one, but I just couldn't do it. I wanted one, but couldn't get over the fact that I felt like I would mess something up.

I shut the fridge and paced back and forth through the kitchen a few times, still calling out for Carrie. That's when I realized her car wasn't there; I somehow never noticed it when I rushed into the house.

I sat on the couch and pondered what to do. I was sore and tired and felt a headache beginning to form after everything that happened today but beyond all that I felt energized, like an incredible weight had been lifted off my shoulders.

I took my shoes off, wincing when my socks came away bloody from the rocks that had torn through the soles of my shoes. I unbuttoned my shirt and leaned back on the couch, closing my eyes and trying to think of what to do next. I had just about dozed off when the phone rang, startling me awake again.

I stood up and stumbled over toward my phone, nearly tripping over the coffee table as I walked. "Carrie?" I answered.

"No buddy, it's Bryce. Is Carrie ok?"

"I don't know, why do you ask?" I responded.

Bryce said "I don't know I just assumed she wasn't there since you asked for her when you answered."

"She's not here, I'm not sure where she went actually." I looked back into the empty hallways and shook my head, coming back to the conversation at hand. Sorry man, whats up?"

"Nothing Jeff, just calling to check on you guys. How's everything?" Bryce inquired.

I paused for a minute before answering. "Why don't you come over here because I need to tell you something."

"Is everything okay Jeff, you sound shaky?" Bryce asked very curiously.

"I'm fine, everything's fine, I may be a little shaky, I just need to talk to you so get here as soon as you can.

I hung up and walked back to the bedroom to change into a clean set of clothes. I looked back at Peyton's picture, smiled and walked out, turning the light off behind me.

Chapter 6

It wasn't long before Bryce's headlights appeared in the driveway, casting shadows across the walls as he pulled to a stop.

A few seconds later he burst through the door, concern written all over his expression. "What's going on, Jeff? You're freaking me out here."

I walked over to him and put a hand on his shoulder. "Nothing is wrong, buddy, nothing at all."

"You sure? I haven't seen you this jumpy since Peyton died and now you're telling me you don't know where Carrie is and I don't know, Jeff, it's hard not to freak out a little."

I just shook my head and nodded toward the couch. "Sit down Bryce, I'll get you a beer and fill you in."

I reached in the fridge and grabbed two beers, walking back into the living room and passing one to Bryce. "Listen, Bryce, what I'm going to tell you is going to sound crazy, but trust me when I tell you every word is completely true.

Bryce watched me carefully for a moment before taking a sip of his beer, absently running a hand through his hair as he mentally prepared himself for whatever I was about to tell him.

"I went out to get some bourbon earlier today and when I left I just started driving, no place in particular, and somehow I ended up back at The Cover." "And?" he asked as he interrupted me.

"Well, I went back to the spot where I found Peyton and I was searching around for...I don't know, anything that made it not real or something that would help me understand that it wasn't my fault."

"And....." I paused, I didn't know how to say the next part. I was starting to sweat a little and could feel my heartbeat quicken. My palms were clammy and my voice felt like it was going to crack if I talked.

"Jeff, what happened? You can tell me." Bryce assured me.

"Well I was wandering through the forest, searching for I don't even know what, and then I heard something."

"You heard something?" Bryce repeated.

I hesitated again, still on the fence about telling him, but I finally choked past the lump in my throat and said "Yeah, I heard Peyton!"

Bryce's eyes widened and he leaned forward in the recliner a bit. "You heard Peyton? Jeff, that's absurd, I know you..."

I interrupted, "No, Bryce, you don't understand, this was real. I know it sounds crazy but it was real."

Bryce sat his beer on the coffee table and shook his head. "Jeff, I know you and Carrie have been struggling with this and I cannot say that I know what you're going through, but Peyton is gone buddy. He died that night and I know a part of you did too!"

I nodded "You're right, a part of me did die."

"I know you're trying to hang on to anything that even resembles Peyton but you have to know he's not coming back, Jeff. It's time to let go and move on.

A little fire in my stomach grew; I wasn't angry or upset, but that fire smoldered in me and grew hotter. I stood up and said "Bryce, you're my brother and I love you but I'm gonna have to ask you to shut up and never say those things to me again. You weren't there, and you have no clue how it feels to lose someone that you were supposed to protect."

Bryce shook his head sadly. "Jeff, I know that…"

I stopped him again. "No, let me speak. What I'm going to tell you is going to be hard to comprehend, I understand that, but you have a choice to make: either try and believe me or go home and I will never speak of this again."

Bryce stood up and said "Jeff, what the hell is happening?"

The more I spoke, the more certain I became that what I had experienced was real. "I don't know exactly what is happening here Bryce, but I do know that I need you to either get on board or go home. What's it going to be?"

He looked at me carefully like he was trying to determine if I'd actually lost my mind or not before finally nodding. Okay, Jeff, okay." He took a sip from his beer and sat back down on the recliner.

"Tell me what exactly happened." Bryce said.

"Okay, like I said, I'm not sure what it all means but when I was out at The Cover I heard Peyton's voice and then I noticed this bright circle of light off in the trees."

"A circle of light?" Bryce asked. "That's weird considering the amount of tree cover and shade in that area…"

"I know, that's what I thought at first, too. I knew I had to check it out so I walked toward it and that's when I heard Peyton again. At first I thought someone was in the woods messing with me, but I shouted and shouted and the only response I ever got was from Peyton."

I could see that Bryce was having trouble accepting what I was telling him but, to his credit, he sat still and kept listening.

"It freaked me out and I took off running through the woods. I kept thinking I would turn back and the light would be gone but when I finally did look back the circle of light was still there. I had to go back, Bryce; I don't know what it was, but it kept me from leaving, I had to know. When I got back I heard Peyton again."

"What did he say, Jeff?" Bryce asked.

"He said 'Dad, November 17th.'"

Bryce looked stunned and repeated, "November 17th?"

"Yeah, that's all that was said. I begged for him to say something else, I wanted to talk to him so bad! It was my son, Bryce, I heard my son out in the woods today."

Bryce put his hand over his mouth and I could tell he was shaking.

I kept talking, pacing around the living room restlessly. "Look, I know this sounds crazy but I'm not making this up. It's weird but after hearing Peyton's voice today I feel like I have an obligation of some sort, some kind of calling that I didn't know about until today."

Bryce asked "What kind of obligation could you possibly have from this?"

I stopped pacing and considered the question for a moment before shaking my head. "I don't know, Bryce. Sometimes things happen in life that can't be explained. They just happen and we all just go with the flow never really asking questions. Well this time I'm asking questions. Something took place out there that awful night and I just took it. And again today something happened out there and this time I'm not going to sit back and just let it go. I'm telling you I ended up back at The Cover today for a reason and I'll spend the rest of life trying to figure out what that reason is if that's what it takes."

Tears had begun to well in my eyes as I finished speaking and Bryce stood up and walked over to me, placing a comforting hand on my shoulder. "Okay Jeff," he said somberly. "I believe you. If you feel that strongly about it, then let's do it. Let's figure out what's going on."

I scrubbed at my face, somewhat surprised by my brother's response. "You really believe me?"

"Yes, I do. I believe you really experienced something that can't be explained and if you believe there's a reason behind it then I do too. I may not understand what you saw or heard but you have my support."

I smiled, a sudden wave of dizziness and relief washing through me. "Thanks man, you have no idea how much that means to me."

Bryce nodded and said "Okay, so what do we do now?"

I sighed and shrugged. "Well, I guess we have to go out and see if it happens again or if we can get anymore information about the original message. I mean, he said November 17th, that date has no significance to Carrie and I. Does it to you?"

Bryce shook his head and shrugged his shoulders.

"So I say we go out again tomorrow and see what happens."

"You want me to go with you?" Bryce asked.

"Yes, that way if you hear it then I'm definitely not crazy." I said grinning.

Bryce grinned back and responded "Okay deal. As crazy as this sounds I have to admit I'm intrigued."

"Alright, so let's meet up here tomorrow and we'll drive out to The Cover together."

"Sounds good," Bryce said as we made our way to the front door. "I'll meet you here after lunch and we'll go from there." Bryce waved over his shoulder as he stepped outside, keys jingling in his hand as he shut the door behind him. I watched from the window as he got back in his car, his headlights flickering on a few seconds later. I waited until he backed out of the driveway, the lights of his car fading in the distance, before turning back and sinking down onto the couch.

For a long time I just sat there, staring at the wall and thinking of all the possibilities that loomed ahead.

I felt peace and tranquility for the first time in a long time. I smiled and leaned back against the couch cushions, ready to call it a night, when I noticed the untouched beer bottle on the coffee table. I had taken one out for myself but I never drank it, never touched it. I picked it up, walked into the kitchen, and poured it out in the sink.

It was the first day I hadn't drowned my sorrows with a bottle since Peyton died.

Smiling, I walked back to the couch, laid down, and fell asleep almost instantly.

Chapter 7

I woke early the next morning and jumped off the couch, sprinting to the bathroom to get ready for the day.

I felt great, in fact I haven't felt this good in a while. The sun beamed in through the windows and I swear the birds chirping outside were chirping directly to me.

I didn't have a headache or any sort of hangover and sobriety was coursing through my veins bringing a feeling of serenity long lost in my world. After using the restroom I splashed some water on my face and brushed my teeth. I looked in the mirror and what leered back at me wasn't sadness, it wasn't guilt or angst, no it was only described as normalcy. It was the first time in years that the image I saw in the mirror didn't embarrass me. The dark circles and bags under my eyes weren't there, the sadness that loomed over me like a cloud had dissipated. And, not knowing what lay ahead, I still mustered up a sly smile.

I called out for Carrie but I didn't get an answer so I walked over to the bedroom and saw she was sleeping peacefully. I wasn't sure when she came home or how long she had been asleep but it didn't matter, I was just relieved to see her. I wanted to tell her about what had happened in The Cover but I also didn't want to wake her so I gathered some clothes from the dresser and stepped out of the room quietly, closing the door behind me.

After I got dressed, I looked out the window and noticed Bryce's car pulling in the driveway. I grabbed my keys and met him outside.

"Good morning, buddy," I greeted Bryce as he stepped out of the car.

Surprised, he smiled and said "wow, someone's feeling good this morning."

I hugged him and said "Bryce, I haven't felt this good in two years. Now let's get going."

Bryce smiled at me as we both slid into his ugly orange car. We pulled out of the driveway and sped off to The Cover. We didn't speak at all, probably from anxiety or anticipation or hell, it could've just been plain nerves. I wasn't sure if I was nervous or scared or excited; I just knew that I had something to accomplish.

Eventually we pulled up to the parking spot where we always left the cars when we went to The Cover and parked. We both took deep breaths to steady our nerves before stepping out.

I looked over and said "Listen, I don't know what's going to happen out here, but I really appreciate you doing this."

Bryce put his hand on my shoulder, squeezed it, and just nodded; he knew how important this was to me. We got out of the car and headed to The Cover.

It was a gorgeous day, a slight breeze swayed through the tree tops and the birds soared with the wind. We got to the top of the hill and I could see the spot where Peyton died. I felt my heartbeat quicken and my pulse in my temples, my hands immediately started sweating.

"You okay, Jeff?" Bryce asked.

"Yeah, being here just brings up a lot of emotions, you know? Anger, fear, sadness. When I see this place, all those emotions come rolling in all at once."

He patted my back and we walked ahead over to where Peyton was found.

"Right here Bryce, right here." I said, pointing at the ground.

"This is where you heard him?" Bryce asked.

"No, this is where he landed after the lightning strike. He hit this tree and that's what killed him." I looked over at Bryce and he had his hand over his mouth, tears welling in his eyes as he looked at the location where Peyton was killed. I could still hear my heart pounding and kept wiping my hands clean from the clamminess.

I looked at the spot for a minute until I couldn't take it anymore and stood, turning back to Bryce. "Okay, right over here was where the light was."

Bryce and I walked over toward the place where I had seen the light. "There was a perfect circle of light right over here and that's when I heard Peyton say November 17th."

"Okay, so what do we do now?" Bryce questioned.

"I don't really know buddy, I don't really know."

We sat there for a while, listening carefully and checking the trees for any sign of light or movement.

Nothing happened.

We stepped away from the clearing and walked over to the pond, tossing rocks into the still, calm water and reminiscing about the good times we'd had in the past when we visited The Cover. For so long it felt like the only thing I remembered about The Cover was Peyton's death but it felt good to remember the other good memories we had here too.

We had been there now for about four hours now and still nothing happened. We heard nothing and saw nothing and I was now convinced I had hallucinated the entire thing. I had worked myself up to believe what I heard and saw and truly thought something would happen again.

Bryce must have seen the disappointed look on my face because he eventually spoke up. "Look, Jeff, just because nothing happened today doesn't mean that nothing happened yesterday, or that it won't happen again. Maybe it's because I'm here, who knows."

"No Bryce, I'm really starting to think I made it up somehow. Maybe it was the alcohol or maybe just grief but I'm starting to think it was all just a figment of my imagination. But you know what? It's okay; I mean I'm disappointed, sure, but it will be okay. Maybe the message was meant for me and only, or maybe I just conjured it up because I was so desperate to hear my son's voice again.".

I shook my head, pulling myself out of my thoughts. "Hey, let's go get a burger and a beer. what you think about that?"

Bryce nodded but continued to look out over the clearing like he was still expecting to see something. "Jeff, I thought about what you told me and I really do think something happened here, I don't think you made it up. I watched your face last night and I know you couldn't be making this up. So don't for a second think that you're crazy, or that I don't believe you. Like you said, sometimes things happen that we can't explain. Come on, let's go get that burger."

We turned and walked toward the car, both breathing sighs of relief almost. My heart had slowed and the cold sweat that plagued me had long since passed. I was disappointed but strangely I was also at peace too. It was all gonna be okay; somehow I knew that.

We started our descent down the hill and then I heard Bryce gasp. "Oh my god!"

I felt my stomach clinch and whipped back around. "What is it?"

He was white as a sheet and his hands were trembling and I saw him point back towards The Cover. I turned my head to look back and my knees buckled a little. The perfect circle of light had appeared right where we had been standing only a few minutes before.

Bryce was still paralyzed, rooted to the spot where he stood as he continued to stare at the light in disbelief. I gathered myself and ran over to the light, desperate to reach in before it disappeared again.

"Peyton!" I yelled out as I got closer, calling his name two or three more times only to hear it echo through the trees around us. I started to get frustrated at the lack of response but the light remained where it was, glowing as brilliantly as ever.

Bryce finally broke himself out of his trance and made his way over to me, planting a hand on my shoulder as he continued to stare at the light. "God, it's beautiful isn't it?" He asked but I didn't answer, I was focused on Peyton. We both stood and looked at the light but never heard anything.

We stood there for a long time and I had just about given up on the idea that we would hear anything when Peyton's voice carried out through the trees. "Dad, nine thirty pm"

I fell backwards and crashed into Bryce, sending us both tumbling to the ground. Peyton's voice was heavenly and rang out like someone shouting from the mountains.

"Peyton son, what are you trying to tell me?" I yelled out as I stood back up, dusting the dirt off of my hands.

"Dad, nine thirty pm" his voice boomed out again.

Bryce stood still like a statue with his hands cupped over his mouth, while I kept yelling out "Peyton, what does that mean? What are you trying to tell me?"

His voice sounded so close I felt like I could reach out and grab him. I wasn't scared; the only thing running through my mind is that I have to do something. I had to find out why this was happening and what my son was trying to tell me.

I yelled out again, "Peyton, please tell me what I need to do!"

I got no answer except his voice repeating, "nine thirty pm." After this, the circle of light disappeared and The Cover returned to normal.

I spun around to see Bryce sitting on his knees, weeping quietly. I ran over to him and fell to my knees beside him, placing a comforting hand on his shoulder as tears continued to stream down his face.

Eventually his tears subsided and he sat there, sniffling miserably for a few moments. "Well, I definitely believe you now," he joked, smiling through his tears.

I smiled as well and helped him up. Taking one last look at the clearing, we turned and made our way back to the car again.

The ride back to the house was as silent as it had been when we left that morning. It was only when we pulled into the driveway that Bryce spoke again. "I think we need to keep this between us for now."

"Why?" I asked.

"I think we need to figure out what Peyton needs from us first before we tell anyone else what happened. He obviously wants you to do something for him and the more people involved might interfere with whatever he's asking of you." He went silent for a second as if debating his next words carefully. "That includes Carrie."

I wanted to protest that, Carrie deserved to know that I was somehow able to communicate with Peyton again, but finally decided he was right. Telling Carrie could either make things better or much worse.

"Okay, you're right. The more people who know, the more complicated things will be. We'll keep this between us until we figure out what the deal is."

"What do you think it all means?" Bryce asked after a moment.

I shook my head. "He said nine thirty pm. And yesterday he said November 17th. So I think he wants us to do something on November 17th at nine thirty pm."

"Any idea what?"

I shook my head again; nothing came to mind.

Bryce shook his head and shrugged his shoulders. "Maybe it's a test, maybe he wants you to keep coming out there. Maybe God is using Peyton to test your faith."

I laughed softly and shook my head. "Who knows? We have to go back out there tomorrow and see if it happens again. I mean November 17th is only a few weeks away so the more messages we get the more we will know."

Bryce nodded and we both understood what we needed to do. I hugged Bryce and got out of his car and walked towards the garage.

The stars glittered overhead and I looked up at them and smiled. I walked inside and shut the door to the night.

Chapter 8

The next morning I woke up feeling even better than I did the day before. The weight of grief and guilt I'd been carrying around for the past two years was gone and I felt like I could finally breathe again. All the soreness and stiffness I'd felt from my tumble in the forest a few days earlier was gone and I was filled with excitement and energy.

I went to the bedroom to grab some fresh clothes and noticed Carrie was gone, the bed neatly made like she'd never slept in it. That was odd but I didn't put too much thought into it, grabbing my clothes from the dresser and stepping into the bathroom to get dressed. I heard a car door shut outside and looked out the window to see Bryce walking up the driveway.

"Morning, bud," I said, stepping out to meet him.

"Morning," Bryce said, looking at the driveway curiously. "Is Carrie not here again?"

"No, I don't think she ever came home last night to be honest with you. I haven't seen her in a couple of days, actually."

"You don't find that weird?"

I shook my head briefly. "She probably went to stay with her mom, she's been staying there a lot recently. We haven't been doing too well lately, both of us too consumed by our grief to really focus on our marriage. When she needs someone to talk to she usually goes over to her mom's house instead of staying here and drowning her pain with alcohol. She'll come back though, I'm sure of it."

We climbed into his car and set off toward The Cover again, both lost in thought as we drove. I had been nervous yesterday, not sure what to expect and what would happen, but today was different. I felt anxious and hurried like I couldn't wait to get there and hear what Peyton would say.

It felt like we couldn't get there fast enough and I had to fight the urge to push Bryce's leg down on the gas pedal so we could get there faster. The turn off finally appeared in the distance and I practically threw myself out of the car as Bryce pulled to a stop.

I sprinted up the hill, leaving Bryce behind at the car. I could hear him yelling behind me, telling me to wait and slow down but I wasn't listening. I kept running until I reached the place where I had heard Peyton's voice the day before. By the time I reached the clearing, I was out of breath and wheezing and I doubled at the waist, my hands gripping my knees as I struggled to breathe.

I looked around for any sign of the light and listened carefully for Peyton's voice but saw and heard nothing.

Bryce slowly made his way up to me as I regained my breath and stood upright. "Where is he?" I asked, more to myself than my brother.

"Just be patient, Jeff," Bryce told me as we walked around the clearing. "I'm sure he'll show up."

I tried to believe him but after walking around for a few hours with nothing I began to feel discouraged. Just as I was about to give up, the light appeared again, just as bright and glorious as it had been before.

"Peyton?" I called out. "Son?"

There was a long pause before he responded. "2466."

That was all he said. Confused, I called out again, "2466? What does that mean, son?"

There was no answer, just that beautiful, shimming light.

I called out once again "Peyton, son, what does that mean? Please tell me!" There was desperation in my voice and my lips quivered a bit as I spoke.

"2466." Peyton's voice echoed through the trees again. Before I could say anything else the light began to fade and was gone again within a few seconds.

I wanted to scream in frustration. I wanted to hear my son's voice again more than anything but I was also very confused about what this message meant.

The other two were somewhat decipherable but this one wasn't at all. I looked over at Bryce and he looked as perplexed as I felt.

Eventually we both seemed to realize nothing else would happen today and started walking towards the car.

It wasn't until we got back on the road that Bryce said, "I think I know what this message means."

I quickly turned my head in his direction "Well by all means tell me because I have no clue what he could be talking about."

"I think it's an address."

"An address?" I repeated.

"Yeah, I really think it's an address he's reading out. 2466, what else could that be?"

I shook my head. "I don't know Bryce."

"You don't have a safety deposit box or a safe that has a combination on it do you?" Bryce asked.

"No, not that I'm aware of. I mean, Carrie could have one but I doubt it."

"Well then what else on God's green earth could it be? He said November 17th then said 930pm and now 2466. I swear he's telling you to go to some place at 930 pm on November 17th."

I was silent for a minute as I thought about what he said. The cryptic messages would make sense if he was telling me to go somewhere but the question I still had was why? What could possibly happen at this address at 9:30 on November 17th? I had no idea but I felt a huge weight lifted from earlier.

"So you think the next message may be the name of the street?" I asked.

"Yes, I do Jeff." Bryce said with a grin on his face.

"Well, I hope you're right and that we hear a street name tomorrow. That would make a lot of sense. But then what do we do when we get there? That's the other big question I have."

"Well, Jeff, I'll be honest with you, I don't think he's going to tell you that."

"What do you mean?" I sharply asked.

"I just have this gut feeling, the way this has all taken place, that he isn't going to tell you what you have to do. You'll just know when you get there." Bryce replied.

I sighed and shook my head again, frustrated with the lack of information.

Bryce continued "Listen, I don't know for sure Jeff, I'm just guessing here, but I do strongly feel that you have something to do and that you're getting tidbits of info so that you stay with it no matter what it is you have to do."

I just stared at him and listened as he spoke. He did make a lot of sense and his comment about God testing my faith was starting to make sense as well. I wasn't a man of faith, not like I used to be, but if this was somehow God's will, if he was using my son's voice to get through to me, I feel like I had no choice but to obey.

I smiled. "You know, I think you could be a preacher if the carpentry thing doesn't work out."

He smiled and waved one hand slightly. "Never thought too much about religion or God, especially after mom and dad died.

But I can't help but feel there's something divine about all this, something we just don't understand yet."

I smiled again and shrugged. "I'm going to go in and grab a bite to eat, you wanna join me?"

"No man, I've got some work to do so I'm going to scram, but I will be here at the same time tomorrow."

I waved as he backed out of the curvy driveway and I turned, startled to see Carrie standing there in the garage. I ran to her and hugged her.

"Where have you been, honey?"

"I went to my mom's for a few days," she told me somberly, hugging me back and resting her chin on my shoulder. "Sorry I didn't tell you, I just needed a couple days to think about things."

"It's okay," I said, walking us both back through the garage and closing the door behind us as we went inside. The house was cold when we entered, neither of us remembering to turn on the heater before we left. I adjusted the thermostat and looked back at Carrie as she grabbed a couple of beers from the refrigerator, holding one out for me.

I shook my head, turning down the beer, and said "so what did you decide?"

She looked confused when I turned down the beer and placed it back in the refrigerator. She looked back at me, took a deep breath, and said, "Jeff, I want us to make this work. I want you in my life especially now, without Peyton, I don't think I could go on living without you."

She sat the beer down and stood up, walking over and cupping my face with her hands. "But things have to change Jeff, we can't keep living the way we have. We don't have sex, we don't sleep in the same bed, hell we don't barely even eat dinner together anymore. I need you, I need my husband, and I'm not going to drink myself to sleep anymore and I don't want you to either."

She brushed her thumb over my cheek. "Do you understand babe?"

I was so overwhelmed, so overcome with emotion I felt like I wanted to climb to the mountain tops and scream it.

"Sit down, sweetie" I said. I kissed her hand as it slid down my face. "I've got something to tell you."

She sat down and looked up at me as she sipped her beer. Her expression was guarded and a little hesitant like she thought I was going to tell her something awful or tell her I was leaving.

I kneeled down in front of her and cupped her hands in mine. "Carrie...I will do whatever you want me to do. I love you and want to be with you too. With Peyton gone, I can't imagine my life without you by my side. I need you too, babe, I can't do this without you."

Tears spilled down her face and I wiped them away with my thumbs, leaning in to kiss her as she wept. We fell into each other's arms, clinging to each other in a way we hadn't done in a long time. We hadn't been intimate with each other since Peyton died and although our grief still lingered like an invisible wound we couldn't stop ourselves once we began. I wanted to tell her so badly, and I was almost going to. But I remembered what Bryce said and it truly made sense. I would tell her one day, or at some point she would find out, but at this moment I would keep it quiet. We sat in the kitchen arms draped in the throws of love and sheer emotions. We ended up in the bedroom, our bedroom, laying together in our bed. Carrie was curled in my arms, her hair spilled out on the pillow behind her, and she was quiet, seemingly lost deep in thought.

I was quiet too; my mind kept wandering around The Cover and the words that Peyton was saying. Once again I almost blurted out what was taking place to her, but as the words were on the tip of my tounuge I bit it and remained silent. A part of me thought she may think I'm crazy or not believe me and it start a fight or I lose her trust.

I knew I needed to tell her but I couldn't, not then. I would tell her everything eventually but I wanted to understand what was happening first.

"I love you," I heard her say quietly, her head snuggled up against my chest.

I kissed the top of her head and pulled her close. "I love you too."

It felt nice, being able to be with each other like this. We'd become so distant for so long, I'd almost forgotten how good it felt to simply hold my wife in my arms. I must have been smiling because Carrie chuckled and reached up, brushing sweat from my forehead.

"What is it?" Carrie asked.

I just shook my head and smiled again. "Nothing honey. I'm just happy again, for the first time in what seems like a lifetime. I'm happy."

I kissed her on the lips and pulled her close, closing my eyes and drifting off to sleep.

Chapter 9

I woke up the next morning feeling better than I had in months. Carrie wasn't in the bed but the sheets were still warm which meant she probably hadn't left that long ago. I sat up and reached over to grab Peyton's picture, holding it close to my heart for a moment before setting it back down. I stood up and slid my shirt on and walked into the living room.

"Carrie?" I called out as I walked through the house, frowning when I got no answer. I wandered into the kitchen and saw a note stuck to the fridge, a few lines written in Carrie's neat handwriting.

She had gone to eat lunch with her mom and sister and wouldn't be back till later that afternoon.

I wandered back to the bedroom to take a shower and when I walked back out I found Bryce sitting in the recliner watching TV. I laughed, "well just make yourself at home buddy."

He chuckled as well and said "well I knocked on the door several times but you didn't answer, so I let myself in."

"I was in the shower," I told him, walking back to the bedroom to retrieve my shoes. I slipped them on and made my way back to the living room, following Bryce out and walking to the car.

Like every day before, we made our way to The Cover and walked back out to the clearing where we'd seen the light and heard Peyton's voice.

As expected, several hours passed with no sign of the light and no sound of Peyton's voice. We waited and walked around, circling the pond a few times and absently tossing a few rocks into the deep still water.

Another hour passed and Bryce and I were about to give up and call it a day. It was cold, the early winter chill creeping up the mountain and turning the air frigid. It was still early November but the sun was beginning to set earlier and the chilly air meant a cold winter ahead.

I had just turned to look at Bryce, ready to suggest we call it an early day, when I caught a flash of light out of the corner of my eye.

Just as before, I ran to it. "Peyton!" I called out.

It stayed silent for a second or two then that booming voice rang out, "Poppy street." His voice echoed through the trees and what little leaves were left rustled as his voice made its way through the forest.

"Okay, son, I hear you. What is it you need me to do?" I pleaded with Peyton to tell me something.

"Dad, Poppy street." Peyton's voice rang out again.

And that was it. Two words and then the light disappeared and The Cover was calm and serene as usual. Bryce walked up behind me, still staring at the spot where the light had been only a few seconds before. "Isn't Poppy street over by the church, you know, that road that goes behind it?"

I hadn't even thought about where that street may be yet; I was only thinking about Peyton and how much I missed him. "Yeah, I think you're right, Poppy street runs behind our church."

"You thinking what I'm thinking?" Bryce asked as we made our way back to the car.

I nodded and patted him on the back as we walked. "You damn right buddy, let's go."

We drove off to find the house matching the information Peyton had given us. We drove for about twenty minutes and turned left into the neighborhood, slowing down to check the numbers on the mailboxes. We drove up and down the street a few times but couldn't seem to find the house.

The road eventually ended in a cul de sac and we began to turn around when I noticed something about one of the houses.

"Wait Bryce, stop."

He hit the brakes and I hopped out of the car, walking toward a rusty old mailbox with overgrowth covering most of it. I moved the weeds away from the mailbox and was just barely able to read the numbers: 2466 and the name read The Wiley's.

"Bryce, this is it," I said excitedly, looking over my shoulder as he got out of the car and walked over to join me. We looked up the driveway that led to the Wiley's house, an ugly, broken down home with junk and trash scattered about the front yard.

The house was stained a dingy yellow and the gutters were rusted, one of them dangled from the left side of the house. A red car sat on blocks in the side yard and a broken down bike without a seat and front tire leaned against it.

The grass was dead and brown so it was hard to tell when the last time it was mowed or even tended to but from the looks of it quite a while. The windows were dirty and dark and there were no screens on them anymore.

Bryce and I stared silently for several long minutes, neither of us believing this could be the place Peyton was telling us about.

"This is it?" Bryce asked like he was confused.

"I suppose, were you expecting something else?" I asked him.

"No, not really. I guess I didn't know what to expect, but I know I didn't expect a run down dump like this."

I nodded and shrugged; this wasn't what I'd been expecting either but I didn't know where else to go. "So I guess I, we, need to come back here at 9:30pm on November 17ᵗʰ?" I asked.

"Sure seems that way, Jeff" Bryce said, still squinting at the house like he was trying to see something that wasn't there.

"What do you think is going to happen?" I heard myself ask. I know he didn't have an answer but I just wanted to hear what he was going to say.

Bryce chuckled and shook his head. "Jeff, if I knew that buddy, I wouldn't be standing here today. I would be on a pulpit somewhere telling people that I could predict the future."

I took a deep breath and nodded. "I hear ya. I guess there's only one way to find out, and that's be here when Peyton is telling us to be here."

We got back in the car and drove off. I looked back at the rundown house one last time as it disappeared behind us and sighed. I had trusted Peyton's message this far but I really couldn't see what he wanted me to do at such a beat up house. I had to believe something was going to happen, that all of this was happening for a reason even if I wasn't sure what that reason was yet.

We pulled into my driveway and I saw that Carrie's car was still gone meaning she hadn't gotten home yet.

"Do you think we should go back out there? I mean, we found the address he told us about." Bryce asked me.

"I don't know, man," I said, shaking my head slowly. "It seems like he's said all he needs to say but I just want to hear his voice again."

"I think he's done, Jeff. He told us everything he needed to tell us and now it's up to us to figure out what it means." He reached over and squeezed my shoulder. "Buddy, I don't know if you're going to hear him again after today."

I knew what Bryce was saying was true but his words still twisted in my gut. The idea of not hearing Peyton's voice again, of never hearing him again, felt almost like losing him all over again. I didn't want to hear it so I interrupted him "Okay, Bryce, well it's been a long day and I'm tired so I'm going to go in and get some grub. If nothing else, I'll see you November17th at 9:30 pm."

Bryce seemed to understand and just nodded, waving at me as I walked up to the house and stepped inside. I shut the door behind me and leaned back against it, closing my eyes tightly. I felt dizzy and uneasy and my mind was cloudy and muddled with thoughts rushing through like a river.

I made my way to the kitchen and got some food, staggering back to the couch and sitting down to watch an old TV show. It was a comedy and the laugh track was a little too exuberant at first but after a while I felt myself beginning to relax as I watched the story play out on screen.

And yes, maybe Bryce was right. I may never hear from Peyton again but for some reason I was okay with that. These past few days had given me solace and I had made peace with this death, something I never would have been able to do had I not gone out to The Cover that day. It wasn't exactly how I imagined it but I felt like I was finally moving forward with my life.

I felt better, more at peace, and was resolved to sit back and let things play out as they were meant to.

Little did I know that things were rapidly about to spiral out of control.

Chapter 10

The first time I met Willis Riley was the next morning when he rang my doorbell.

I was surprised to hear the doorbell ring since Bryce wasn't going to be there for another hour or so. I opened the door slowly to see a bald man with glasses standing on my front porch. He was about mid-forties, short and scruffy with a beard and coffee stains on his teeth and lapel. I could tell he was high strung just by looking at him and he began speaking very fast the second I opened the door. "Are you Jeff Lockler?"

"Yeah, and you are?"

"My name is Willis Riley, I'm a reporter." he said as he stuck his hand out to shake mine.

I shook his hand, noticing the weakness of his grip, and asked, "Well, it's a pleasure to meet you, Mr. Riley, but you still have yet to tell me why you are here?"

He took a sip from a very large cup of coffee and puffed on a cigarette and said, "well sir, I'll cut right to the chase. I had a very interesting conversation with your brother, Bryce, last night. He told me that apparently you can communicate with the dead?"

I froze for a second before quickly pushing him back away from the door and walking out with him, closing the door behind me. I still hadn't told Carrie about any of this yet and I wanted her to hear it from me instead of this guy. "Okay look pal, I have no clue who you are but I don't appreciate you showing up at my house at eight in the morning asking me if I communicate with the dead"

He interrupted me, saying, "look, Mr. Lockler, I spoke with your brother at length last night and he told me the whole story. Now I'm giving you the chance to tell me your side of the story and explain what really happened. And regardless of whether or not you want to talk to me, I've already started writing the article and I have all the info from Bryce so you can come forward and talk to me and help me get this story, or you can sit back and let this transpire because it's going to happen anyway you cut it. He gave me full permission to write it and I'm moving forward with it."

I stared at this man with his empty, soulless eyes and felt white-hot rage in the pit of my stomach. I hated this man and I haven't known him for more than five minutes. Who did he think he was, strolling up to me and pretty much demanding I help him with this story.

"You listen to me you son of a bitch," I growled furiously. "Whatever you think you know, isn't any of your business, and whatever you think you heard, you didn't hear correctly. Also, I know my brother and Bryce would never cooperate with you on anything."

He gave me a smug smile and reached into his pocket. "I believe this is his written statement right here." He pulled out a folded up piece of paper and unfolded it and it was Bryce's handwriting for sure.

I stared at the paper in his hand in disbelief. "Where did you get this?"

Willis sipped his coffee again, smiling maliciously, and said "well your brother struck up a conversation with me last night at a local bar. We started talking and that talk eventually steered towards the afterlife. Where I told him that even if there was an afterlife, there's no way he could prove it. He then proceeded to tell me this story, and it is an incredible story, no question. I figured it might be worth looking into so I thought I'd come talk to you in person. If it happens to be true, you can believe me when I say I'm just the first in a very long, long line of people who will want to speak with you." He gave another smug smile. "And if it's all a hoax, well, I'll make sure the truth comes to light."

It was all I could do to not slug him in the face.

"By the way," Willis continued, flicking his cigarette out into the driveway. "Bryce told me you haven't told your wife about all this yet."

"Yeah so?" I said, shrugging my shoulders.

"Well, why? I mean she's the mother of your child but you felt compelled not to tell her about your miraculous communication with your deceased son?" Willis reached in his pocket and pulled out another cigarette and lit it up. "Basically, Mr. Lockler, I want to know the answers to these questions that I have. And, I'll be honest with you, I want to be proved wrong."

I quickly asked "Proved wrong?"

"Of course! Physical, tangible proof of the afterlife? That's a journalist's dream! You prove to me it exists and you'll never hear from me again. We got a deal?"

He again stuck his hand out for another hand shake and I wanted to rip it off and beat him with it.

I held my composure and asked "What exactly do you need from me?"

"I want to go out there with you to see it for myself. If what your brother said is true and your deceased son speaks to you out in the woods, that's all the proof I'll need." Willis realized I wasn't going to shake his hand and put it back by his side.

"Okay, so I take you out there and that's it? You write your story and then leave me and my family the hell alone? I asked sternly.

"Well obviously, I don't know what the repercussions of this story might be but yes, I will promise that I will leave you alone."

I wasn't sure what to do or think; all I knew was I didn't care for this wiry little guy on my porch and that Bryce needed a stern talking to. I looked back through the window, seeing that Carrie hadn't woke up yet, and then looked back at Willis. "Okay pal, I'll give you your damn story, but on one condition."

"And that is?" he asked.

"You leave my wife and brother out of this. Carrie has been through enough already and I'll tell her about all this when the time comes; until then she's not to be bothered by you or anyone else. Deal?"

This time I stuck my hand out to shake. I truly didn't want to touch this nasty guy, I wanted to spit in his face to be honest, but I held my hand out anyway.

"Deal" he said, shaking my hand. "I'll be back around this time tomorrow and we'll go see if the miracle of the afterlife is real." Willis said as he laughed and tossed his cigarette into the yard.

He got into his van and pulled off into the distance. I watched his broken down, rusted up van get smaller and smaller as it drove away, silently hoping he would crash or get locked up or something that would prevent this all from happening.

My stomach turned and my throat tightened up as I walked back inside the house. I shut the door and leaned against it, wiping the sweat from my head. I slid down the door into a squatting position and put my head between my legs, trying to take a deep breath to calm myself down even though I knew deep down it wouldn't help. That night I barely slept at all and what little sleep I did get was filled with nightmares of the night Peyton was killed.

The next morning I sat at the kitchen table, disheveled and groggy and trying to fight the nerves that were eating away at me. Carrie didn't seem to notice, wandering around the house and gathering her things as she prepared for a meeting up at the church.

"Bye sweetie" she said, kissing my forward as she made her way to the door. It was all I could do to muster a barely audible, "love you" as she stepped out.

After she left I went to the bathroom and put some deodorant on and splashed water on my face. I was making my way back to the cup of coffee sitting on the table when I saw Bryce's car pull into the driveway.

He jumped out and ran up to the house. He burst in a few seconds later, already apologizing. "Jeff, holy crap man, I am so sorry, I am so, so sorry, I never in my life thought that this guy would…"

I interrupted, "So I guess keeping it between you and me didn't mean the same thing huh, Bryce?"

"No, let me explain," he said, holding up his hands pleadingly. "I just went to grab a beer two nights ago and the next thing I know I'm striking up a conversation with this guy who starts bringing up ghosts and religion and the afterlife and all that. I should have just walked away but he was so rude and condescending I just couldn't help it and ended up telling him about what had been going on in The Cover."

I just scoffed and said "I realize that Bryce, but do you understand what you did by telling this guy this stuff? Drunk talk is one thing, but signing a written statement, Bryce, that's something totally different."

"I know man, I know, I'm sorry. In all honesty I thought he was bull shitting when he said he was a reporter. He wasn't wearing a name tag or anything."

"I don't think you realize the ramifications of this, Bryce," I said with a sigh. "I mean this could be very bad."

He sighed and lowered his head. "I feel awful Jeff., The last thing I wanted to do was ruin anything or break your trust. Is there anything I can do to fix this or anything at all?"

"No" I retorted "He'll be back with camera crew and all and I have to escort him to The Cover to prove or disprove the afterlife."

"Well, if we go out there and Peyton gives us another message then it's proven and on camera., That's good right?"

I slammed my coffee cup down on the table, spilling it out the top. If he does give us another message, which I don't think he will, then everyone will know something that I think is meant only for me and you to find out about. And who knows there's a very good possibility that nothing does happen at all and we truly have just been crazy."

"I don't want the whole world to know about this but now there's no stopping it," I continued, irritated. "This is a double-edged sword, Bryce. If something happens out there, the story is going to blow up and go to every major news outlet in the world. If nothing happens, we'll be labeled as frauds. Either way, this incredible, miraculous thing that happened out in The Cover is now shot."

I threw my hands up in the air in frustration and walked off towards the fridge. I opened it up and almost grabbed a beer but I didn't, I grabbed a soda instead.

"I don't know what to think buddy," I said, popping the tab on the soda and taking a long drink. "I truly just want it to be over with, the whole thing."

71

Bryce stood up from his chair and walked over to me, laying a hand on my shoulder.

"I can't tell you how sorry I am, I never meant for this to happen."

I shook my head but didn't look at him. "I know you didn't but it is what it is now. Just gotta get through it."

It hit me, then, that this was the exact same type of feeling, and the same type of conversation I had with Peyton the night he died. It was a strange, eerie feeling, wholly unsettling.

I turned to look at Bryce when the knock on the door startled me. I'd been so caught up in my thoughts I hadn't even realized Willis' beat up van had pulled up into the driveway.

He stood at the door with a cigarette in his mouth and a huge cup of coffee in one hand. Apparently this was his routine, no wonder he was so high strung and didn't ever smell pleasant.

Bryce saw him and bolted out the door to confront him. "You son of a bitch, what the hell are you trying to pull?"

Bryce reached out to grab Willis but Willis backed up quickly and said, "if you lay one hand on me, I will press charges."

Bryce didn't care and tried to take a swing but I grabbed him from behind in a bear hug. "He's not worth it Bryce, just let it be." Bryce took a deep breath and turned to walk away, mumbling under his breath.

I turned back to Willis and growled, "Okay, asshole, let's get this over with. And remember, my wife is not to be involved in this at all."

He nodded and took another drag from his cigarette, tossing the butt into my driveway. "Okay, get in and let's go."

Bryce turned back suddenly. "I'm going, too," he said, walking over to join me in Willis' rusty, old van. Willis looked at me for assurance as he started to climb in the drivers seat. I didn't care if he came with us or not; I knew how this was going to turn out and having Bryce with me wasn't going to change it so I shrugged my shoulders and Bryce and I got it in. We left my house and made our way to The Cover.

Nobody spoke as we drove; Willis sipped his coffee and smoked and the whole van stunk like cigarettes and stale coffee. The back of the van was covered in papers and of course empty coffee cups. His cameraman sat in the back on the floor, and fiddled with his camera. The only time I spoke was to give directions, other than that the entire trip was silent. We finally pulled up to The Cover and got out of that nasty van.

"Okay, time to learn about the afterlife." Willis said as he climbed out of the van.

"We have to hike up the hill a little, but it's not bad. Your cameraman may struggle a little, though."

"He'll be fine," Willis said, nodding for me to lead the way.

I guided them up the hill and toward the clearing where we'd seen the light and heard Peyton's voice. It seemed brighter today which was odd considering how shady The Cover usually was.

We reached the clearing and Willis tossed another cigarette on the ground. and said "Okay, so what happens now? We pray or do some kind of little dance and then we hear your son?"

"No, we do nothing." I said.

"So, where does this miraculous communication usually happen?" Willis asked.

"Right over there,.." I said while I pointed to where the circle of light had appeared all the time before.

Willis' cameraman never uttered a word and went about setting up his camera in that direction. He was an odd man as well, a short and fat man, with a very dark tan. He had a scar that went down his face, from his temple to his throat, and a tattoo on his forearm of a cross. He never spoke but would smile every now and then and I could see he didn't have many teeth. He finished setting the camera up and proceeded to sit down on the ground and wait.

We sat and stood around for a while, nobody speaking. I had to keep an eye on Bryce because he really wanted to take another shot at Willis and honestly, so did I. The only thing stopping me was the possibility of a lawsuit but it wasn't a major deterrent.

After several hours with no communication, I began to get the sinking feeling that Peyton really wouldn't speak up again. Willis would label us as frauds and that would be that. All of a sudden Willis spoke up. "In 1976 I did an interview with this guy that was a journalist and a radical one as well. He was very weird and quirky, and I thought he was on drugs. Well the interview went on and he kept making these outrageous claims and we would have to do another take because we were filming it.

Well I went to use the bathroom and when I returned he had this white stuff on his left hand. I really didn't think too much of it, but when I asked him if he was ready to do another take he said sure and snorted the white stuff on his hand. And then went right into the interview, and he did it better after the coke he snorted. He drank the entire time and wasn't making a whole lot of sense. I eventually ended the interview, shook his hand and we left.

I canned the footage, never showing it to anyone, and I lost my job at that paper because it was such a mess. I couldn't figure out why my boss was so certain that he get interviewed and then he fired me for not getting it. I never could figure it out until a few years later and I read a book by this fella. You know who this was?"

We all looked at each other and shook our heads.

He smiled and said "It was David S. Thompson, and the book I read was about the Devil's Angels. A magnificent piece of writing I may add, but what's funny is that I had interviewed this guy that turned out to be icon in journalism and novella. And I blew it because I hadn't done my research and diligence. So from that moment forward, I vowed to always do my due diligence and research the crap out of everything."

Bryce spoke up "Why are you telling us this?"

"Because I was trying to have a little conversation and also so that you guys know why I'm so persistent and pesky." Willis explained.

"You're pesky and persistent because you're a dick." Bryce said angrily.

"Fine, if you don't want to talk pleasantly then we won't talk at all,." Willis muttered as he lit up another cigarette.

We stood and sat around silent for the next three hours before finally conceding that Peyton wouldn't be showing up to speak with us after all. We waited as the cameraman packed up his gear and then made our way back to the van. The ride back was just as silent as the ride there had been and the smug smile on Willis' face never wavered. We pulled into the driveway and started to get out of the van when Willis spoke. "Well, gentlemen, that was a huge waste of time but, then, I figured it would be. Guess this is goodbye?" Willis said sticking his hand out to be shaken.

I just looked at him and turned around and shut the door.

Bryce and I never looked back at the van as he pulled out of the driveway, we went inside where I laid down on the couch. I was hungry and thirsty but couldn't muster up the energy to make me something.

Bryce said goodbye and I drifted off to sleep.

Chapter 11

The next morning, I woke up with a sick feeling in the pit of my stomach. I wasn't sure why, but it lingered all morning. I couldn't explain it but it was like I knew something bad was going to happen. I poured a cup of coffee and walked out on the front porch. The birds were chirping and the sun was beaming down like little rays of heaven, it was a gorgeous day. Even with the beauty of the day, I couldn't think of anything but Willis Riley.

I couldn't figure out his plan; why did he go to great lengths to get this story when he was sure Bryce and I were making it up? It didn't make any sense and for the life of me I couldn't figure out his motivation behind this story. I soaked up a little more of the day and finished up my coffee, walking back inside and putting my cup in the sink. I showered and got dressed and wandered into the living room, slumping down on the couch and turning on the TV. For some reason I felt like I shouldn't, like I was about to see something upsetting, but I couldn't stop myself. About ten minutes into me flipping through the channels, the twelve o'clock news came on, and low and behold, Mr. Riley himself was standing in front of the cameras.

It was the whole thing, everything from Peyton's death to the footage of us standing out in The Cover, waiting to hear him speak. He ridiculed Bryce and I, calling us hacks and frauds and suggesting we needed professional help. He brought up my alcohol abuse and made light of our marital problems.

I stood there shaking, bile rising in my throat, as I watched Willis Riley tear mine and my brother's reputations to shreds. The phone rang, startling me out of my stupor, and I picked it up without turning my attention away from the story on the screen. "Hey Bryce"

"You saw it too, huh?"

"It's all over the news, Bryce. What the hell are we going to do?" "Jeff, there's nothing we can do about it now. Riley lied to us and now there's nothing to stop him from slandering us all over the news."

"I'm not worried about that," I said, still staring at the screen as Riley continued speaking. "I'm worried that whatever Peyton was trying to tell us won't happen now because it's like we broke his trust. Whatever he was trying to tell us to do, whatever was supposed to happen, it feels like it won't happen now."

"Don't give up hope, Jeff," Bryce said. "Riley's a creep but I still think we're meant to do something with Peyton's message. Let others think what they want; we know what we saw and experienced."

I couldn't think of anything else to say so I just said goodbye slumped back down on the couch. I hoped Carrie hadn't seen the news yet; I wanted her to know what had happened but I wanted to be the one to tell her, not Riley. Part of me wanted to rush out to find her and tell her everything right then but the other part still wanted to wait until I figured out exactly what was going on. November 17th was only a week away and maybe then I could finally get the answers I needed.

I saw her car pull into the driveway and felt a weight settle in my chest as I wondered if she'd heard the news already or not. When she walked in she just smiled and walked into the kitchen to pour herself a glass of wine. "You want one, babe?" she called over her shoulder, no indication of anger in her voice. I felt a wash of relief rush through me and shook my head, walking into the kitchen and pecking her on the cheek. "No thanks, babe, I'm gonna go lay down. It's been a long day." I made sure the TV was off so she couldn't hear it. She was going on a trip today with her Mom and I just prayed that the news wouldn't find her. Her family, most likely, wouldn't hear it on the news living where they lived, I know Bryce wasn't going to tell her, so what I was really worried about was her friends from church, I just wasn't sure. I didn't truly know what to do at all, I was so perplexed, disheveled, you name it I felt it. The feelings bubbled and churned like a shook up soda. I tried to coax Carrie into the bedroom to keep her from watching any TV at all, but I knew she had already packed and was leaving soon.

Carrie seemed a little confused but she didn't try to stop me as I walked out of the room and made my way to the bedroom. I stripped my shirt off as I walked and collapsed onto the bed, staring up at the darkened ceiling and trying to relax enough to go to sleep. Anxiety and doubt still swirled in my chest and I couldn't stop thinking about Riley's interview. I tried my best to drown out his condescending words and rolled over onto one side, closing my eyes and wishing for sleep.

I woke up the next morning with a terrible headache; it felt like I was coming down with something. Carrie was already gone by the time I pulled myself out of bed which was probably just as well because if I looked as awful as I felt she'd probably take me to the hospital. My throat felt scratchy and my chest and sinuses felt heavy and tight like the beginnings of a cold were setting in.

I put on the coffee pot and then wandered into the bathroom to find some cold medicine, downing it dry and gulping hard to swallow. I turned and made my way back down the hall, slumping onto the couch and turning on the TV. I just hoped that stupid news story wasn't still airing.

I must've fallen asleep watching TV because the next thing I remember was Bryce was shaking me awake.

"What, what?" I mumbled groggily, confused at who was shaking me.

"Did you drink last night?" Bryce asked.

I sat up, coughed, and shook my head. "No, I took some medicine and I guess it knocked me out. I feel like shit."

"Well, you look like it too," Bryce said, concern coloring his expression. "You weren't answering your phone so I came to check on you. I wanted to make sure that asshole's news story wasn't bumming you out too bad."

I wrapped myself up in a blanket and sniffed miserably. "I thought you told me not to let is bother me."

"Yeah, but I knew it would bother you regardless so I came over," Bryce said with a chuckle.

I shrugged and coughed again. "Well, like you said, it is what it is. No reason to let it suffocate me."

Bryce smirked and patted me on the back. "Glad to see you take my advice for once," he said, nodding to the door. "Let's go get a burger and beer, huh?. You may feel better getting out and about for a few."

I didn't feel like going anywhere honestly but relented and stood up to go to the bathroom and get cleaned up. I felt like warmed over poop, body ached, throat sore, just crappy. But reluctantly I threw some fresh clothes on and we jumped in Bryce's car and headed for the restaurant.

It was a beautiful day and the waitress who greeted us at the door was chipper and friendly and I hated that I felt so under the weather. Bryce ordered a beer and a glass of water and I asked for coffee because in spite of the bright, beautiful day, it was chilly outside and I felt like I was freezing sitting inside the restaurant.

I hadn't noticed it at first but the waitress kept giving us strange looks when she passed by our table. Not in a rude way but in a sly *I know you from somewhere* kind of way.

I nudged Bryce and nodded over to her. "Do you see that?"

"What?" he replied.

I pointed at our waitress. "The three women over there, they're all talking and whispering and every time I look over there they turn away."

Bryce snickered and looked back at them over his shoulder. "Maybe they think we're cute."

I rolled my eyes. "I doubt that."

Bryce started to turn and look again but just then our waitress walked up with our food. "Can I get y'all anything else?" she asked as she set the plates down on the table. We both shook our heads and she took about three steps back before stopping and turning back to us. "Okay, please forgive me for asking this, but are you two guys they were talking about on the news last night?"

I shook my head. "Listen, sweetheart, I'm sure you're a great girl and all but this really isn't something either of us want to talk about."

"Right, of course," she said, obviously flustered. "Just one thing, though."

"Yes?" I said.

"Did you really hear your dead son's voice?"

I couldn't contain my irritation any longer and got up, pushing past her to the door and leaving my untouched food on the table. I didn't even care if I hadn't paid for my meal or not.

My eyes started watering the second I stepped outside but I wasn't sure if it was from the brightness of the sun or the cold I'd caught. I started toward Bryce's car but stumbled to a stop when I saw three or four reporters hovering nearby, their cameras locked on me as I approached. All at once they all rushed forward, all speaking at the same time. "Mr Lockler, is it true, did you think you heard voices from the grave?"

"Did you really hear your son's voice?"

"Do you believe in the afterlife, Mr. Lockler?"

My heart was thudding in my chest as I pushed my way through the sea of cameras and people trying to make it the car. I was angry and irritated and dizzy but my only focus was getting inside the car and hopefully drowning out the piercing drone of the questions.

I felt someone come up behind me and thought for a brief moment I was about to get into a fight with one of the reporters but quickly realized it was just Bryce. He pushed us both forward through the mob of reporters and practically threw me into the car, climbing into the driver's seat a few seconds later.

He sped out of the parking lot so quickly his tires started to smoke a little. I remember thinking he was going to hit one of the reporters as we sped away from the restaurant but luckily he never did. "Holy crap man," Bryce muttered as he drove. "Holy crap, I never expected that!" That was crazy."

I let my head fall back against the headrest and closed my eyes. I felt awful and I just wanted to go back home. Bryce kept talking, mostly to himself, asking over and over how they all found out, how they found us, what they wanted. I never answered, I just kept my eyes closed and struggled to keep my breathing under control.

The whole ride home was a blur and I was dismayed to find a couple of reporters waiting in the driveway when we got back to the house. Bryce parked and rushed around to my side of the car, scooping me out of the front seat and rushing me to the door like a bodyguard. I was exhausted and sick and overwhelmed and by the time I made it to the couch I was weeping openly. Bryce, however, was pissed. He called the police as soon as we got inside and demanded they send someone over to break up the swarm of reporters in front of the house. I heard him talking, his voice angry yet distant in my aching head, and it felt like this was all some kind of awful nightmare.

Eventually the police arrived and managed to disperse the crowd, hanging back to get the full story from Bryce before they left. Again, I heard all of this but it felt like it was drifting in and out of my consciousness like a dream. When the police finally left, Bryce walked over to the couch and shook his head. "Man, you look terrible. Why don't you go get some rest and I'll keep an eye on everything out there."

I nodded and stood up and began shuffling my way back to the bedroom when Bryce's voice stopped me. "Hey Jeff?"

"Yeah buddy?"

"We gotta tell Carrie what's going on."

My heart sank into my stomach. I knew I had to tell her what was going on but I wasn't sure how, especially since I still wasn't sure why this was all happening. She deserved to know the truth though, there was no denying that. "I'll just tell her when she gets home,." I mumbled back, shuffling down the hall again toward the bedroom. That had been my plan, at least. I shrugged my shoulders and went and crawled in bed. It felt good to lay down in the bed, a place I had slept only three or four times now since Peyton had died. But for the second time in as many days I drifted off to sleep in that bed, very weary of what lie ahead.

A couple of days had went by and I still had managed to not tell Carrie about the whole thing. I was scared to death to tell her, would she believe me, would she not believe me? I didn't know, the only thing I did know was that I was terrified to tell her. She hadn't been home for a while, almost a week. She had called a few times and I was just waiting for the "well Jeff you gonna tell me about the news report I heard?" But it never came.

Her mom and sister took her on a beach trip to Puget Sound so that had helped me not telling her. And of course that helped her not hearing about the T.V. thing that had ran and made a mockery of Bryce and I. I knew I had to tell her but I was hoping to not have to tell her until the whole thing was over. If and when it would ever be over, I wasn't sure if it would. But something kept telling me to wait and whether it would come crashing down or I would tell her and it would be almost divine.

Before I knew it, it was November 17th, the date Peyton had indicated in his message.

With everything that had happened with Willis Riley and the rapid reporters I had completely forgotten about the upcoming date until it was already there. I felt a wave of excitement and anxiety sweep through me at the thought that this could all be over soon, that I could finally know what was going on. With a burst of energy, I hurried to the shower to get cleaned up. I still wasn't sure what to expect today but I knew I should be ready for anything. By the time I got dressed and walked back into the living room Bryce was sitting on the couch waiting for me.

I sat on the couch and put my shoes on, glancing at the clock on the wall. It was a little after 8pm which meant in about an hour and a half we should expect something to happen on Poppy street across town.

"It took us about 30 minutes to reach Poppy street last time so we should leave here around 8:45 if we want to be there on time," I told Bryce as I finished tying my shoes.

He nodded and we both waited in nervous anticipation until we couldn't stand it any longer and walked out the door at 8:39.

The ride there was silent, neither of us knowing what to say about whatever fate lay ahead of us. Whatever Peyton was trying to tell me, whatever he wanted me to do, it had something to do with that beat up, run down house at the end of Poppy street. Could all this really just be nonsense, or was something really gonna take place?

We had just topped the hill when we saw the flames in the distance, glowing bright and hot in the cold, dark November night. Bryce pulled to a stop and we took a second to look at each other before jumping out and rushing toward the burning house.

I took off running up the hill, slipping a few times as my shoes slid in the damp grass. I could feel the heat from the flames as I got closer and the fire was so bright it was nearly blinding.

Over the roar of the flames, I heard the sound of a woman screaming for help.

It was faint but still very distinct and before I knew what I was doing I was bursting through the front door and rushing inside. The heat was almost unbearable but I didn't care; I just knew I needed to help the woman trapped inside. I heard the scream again and followed it down a dark, smoke-filled hallway. My eyes and throat were burning and I pulled my shirt over my mouth in a desperate effort to breathe past the smoke. I heard another scream and pushed open the door to a bedroom to see a panicked young woman laying on the ground.

The roof had partially collapsed, pinning one of her legs to the bed and preventing her from moving. She was coughing violently and had tears streaming down her cheeks as I approached. "Ma'am, I'm going to get you out of here!, Put your gown over your mouth so you can breathe." I screamed to her over the roar of the flames.

She shook her head and pointed toward the hall. "Don't worry about me!, My son is in the bedroom down the hall!." My heart sank and I didn't know what to do. If I left her here she would surely die but if I saved her and left her son, he would perish too.

Just then Bryce burst into the room and rushed over to the bed. "I got her," he told me, shoving me back toward the door. "Go!"

I staggered back, leaving him with her, and ran straight to the kid's room, kicking open the door.

The boy was unconscious in the bed, overcome by the smoke that filled his room, and he hung in my arms limply when I picked him up. I turned back toward the door only to see that the flames had now filled the hallway, blocking our exit. A flash of despair swept through me and for a brief second I feared we were trapped. I wasn't about to go down without a fight though and turned to the window instead.

Rust had sealed the window closed but the glass shattered with one well placed kick. I held the unconscious boy close and dove out the window, slamming into the grass outside and knocking the breath out of me. My lungs were still burning and I was coughing so much I could barely breathe but I managed to pull myself up and drag the boy away from the burning house.

I fell to my knees beside him and discovered to my horror that he wasn't breathing. I pressed my fingers to his throat but couldn't find a pulse either. I shook my head, refusing to believe it was too late, and started pumping his chest furiously, only pausing occasionally to give him mouth-to-mouth. Time seemed to slow and I could feel my arms beginning to burn as I kept pumping his chest but I refused to stop. Still, the longer it went without any results, the more my hope began to fade.

Finally, I heard a weak cough and then the boy was choking and gasping as he struggled to breathe. I laughed with relief and rolled him over onto his side, patting his back solidly to help him catch his breath. "Are you okay, son?"

He coughed and coughed and finally managed to nod.

I could hear sirens in the distance, wailing loud and clear in the cold night and felt a wave of relief. I glanced back at the boy, still coughing and choking on the ground, and felt my own body begin to sink down as well. The exhaustion, the smoke, the whole experience had literally almost killed me. My eyes rolled back and then I knew nothing more.

Chapter 12

It was the second time I'd woken up in the hospital since Peyton died and the thought settled with a sick feeling in the pit of my stomach. The fluorescent lights were bright enough to give me a headache and my throat was raw and painful.

There was an IV hooked into one arm and bandages around my arms and legs from where the glass had cut into me when I dove out the window. I remembered a little bit of what happened but most of it was a blur. I remember the flames and the woman screaming and rescuing her son but that was about it. Apparently I inhaled more smoke than I'd originally thought because I had a oxygen mask placed around my mouth and nose to help me breathe and several of the machines next to my bed were monitoring my oxygen levels.

My skin felt tight and hot on my legs and a cursory glance told me I hadn't made it out of the burning house without getting a few burns of my own. Luckily they looked pretty superficial and would probably heal in a few days.

A doctor entered the room a few seconds later and smiled when he saw I was awake.

"How's Bryce," I asked, my voice sounding hoarse and rough from all the smoke I inhaled. "How's my brother? Did he get out, where is he? Is he…"

The doctor interrupted me. "He's fine. He sustained a few injuries but he's expected to make a full recovery."

I let out a relieved sigh which inevitably turned into a hoarse cough. A nurse came over to the bed and raised it up into a slight incline which helped me breathe easier. While this was going on, I glanced toward the door and saw a young woman peaking into the room.

She was young, late twenties probably, but there were lines around her eyes and mouth that made it seem like life had aged her more than her years. She wiped her eyes a few times as she watched me like she was trying to hide tears but I couldn't understand why. It then dawned on me who she was, this was the woman from the house.

I leaned onto my side, grimacing in pain, and motioned for her to come in.

The nurse noticed her and gently said, "ma'am you can't be in here right now. I need to ask you to leave."

The woman started to back out again but I stopped her. "No, it's fine. Please let her stay, I want to talk to her!"

I wasn't sure what to say, or what to expect her to say, but I knew I wanted to talk to her. She was a plump woman, short in stature but robust with size. Didn't matter though she was cute as a button with her curly blond hair and stunning blue eyes.

The doctor nodded to the nurse and they both walked to the door. "Just don't stay too long, he still needs to rest," the doctor told the woman as he passed, carefully closing the door behind him.

For a moment the woman didn't move, standing hesitantly over in the corner like she couldn't decide if she wanted to sit or stay standing. Eventually she walked over to the bedside and pulled up a cushioned chair that had been pushed up against the wall.

We sat in silence for a minute, the woman fiddling with the hem of her shirt nervously. Finally I broke the silence. "So what's your name?"

"Olivia," she answered "Olivia Banks"

"Olivia Banks, huh? That's a pretty name."

"My son, Allen, well…" she started but broke into tears. My heart froze thinking she was about to tell me he didn't make it. "You saved his life. You saved both of our lives," she said through tears.

I reached over and grabbed her hand, squeezing it comfortingly.

"Sir-" she started to say but I cut her off gently.

"Jeff," I said "Please call me Jeff."

She wiped her eyes and said, "Jeff, you could have been killed. Why would you risk your lives for us? You've never met us before in your life." I looked at her and said "Well, we weren't just going to just sit there and leave you there to die." She again started crying and kept squeezing my hand. Eventually the doctor opened the door and said quietly, "I'm sorry to break this up but he really needs to rest now." Olivia nodded and stood, pushing her chair back against the wall. She smiled at me, huge tears still in her eyes, and took a step toward the door. "I uh…I tried to go speak with your friend but he was still asleep. I wanted to thank him too."

She moved toward the door again but I stopped her. "Olivia?" She turned back to look at me.

"Could I meet your son tomorrow?" I asked, suddenly nervous for reasons I couldn't explain. "I mean, if he's awake that is."

She smiled and nodded, those huge tears in her eyes now streaming down her cheeks. "Yes, I would love that." She reached for the door and looked back at me one last time. "Thank you again for saving our lives."

She had almost shut the door when she turned back one last time. "Can I ask you one more quick question Jeff?"

"Sure Olivia."

"How did you guys know to be there at that exact moment? I mean of all the streets and houses in that neighborhood, how did you know to come to ours?"

I just shrugged my shoulders. "Right place, right time I guess."

She smiled and said "No sir, I think you were meant to be close enough to get there in time to help us. It's almost like you were told to be there." She smiled again and stepped out, closing the door behind her. Her words bounced around in my head like a ping pong ball and suddenly it all made sense. Peyton's message, the date, the street, all of it; it all had to do with this family. This is what Peyton was telling us, and it occurred to me too that Bryce had to be there, it was meant for him to be there so they both could survive.

A wave of emotion swept through me then and I was beaming with tears rolling down my face. I still couldn't explain it but I knew this was what Peyton meant for us to do. I laid back against the pillows and closed my eyes, suddenly exhausted, and started to drift off to sleep.

Just before I fell asleep, however, it dawned on me...Olivia said her son's name was Allen and Allen had been Peyton's middle name. This was truly divine!

Chapter 13

The next morning I was awakened by the same doctor from the night before coming in to check on me. He ran a few tests and, satisfied with the results, told me I could be released the next day. My wounds and burns would heal and there didn't appear to be any lasting damage to my body. I had lacerations down my back from the glass and minor burns and scrapes, and of course acute smoke ventilation but was expected to make a full recovery. Just as the doctor was stepping out I heard a familiar voice beside me. "Did you sleep well?"

I jumped a little; I hadn't even seen Carrie next to me when I first woke up. I smiled and reached over to take her hand. "When did you get here?"

Carrie smiled and pulled my hand up to her lip, kissing my knuckles gently. "I got here around three in the morning. You were sleeping and I didn't want to wake you."

"Why didn't you go home and sleep?"

"I wasn't going anywhere except right next to you." Carrie responded with a smile, her eyes brimming with tears. "You're a hero, baby, you saved that woman and her son." I grinned and shook my head. "I wouldn't say hero, just the right place at the right time."

She shook her head and said "You and Bryce are heroes whether you want to be modest or not. Those people would have died had you not been there." She smiled again and wiped the tears from her eyes. "And Peyton always did say you were his hero."

I almost broke down when she said that, but remained calm. and said "Well then you're my angel, Carrie."

She stood and kissed me, sniffling a little as she sat back down. "Will you please tell me the whole story one day?"

I whispered back, "of course, angel." She sat back down and I asked her "how did you know about this?"

"There was a phone call from a woman that said you were in the hospital. She was course and brash and refused to give me an info. So I went to the hospital and finally a lovely doctor told me the whole story. So that's how my dear, that's how." She said somberly but proudly.

I was nervous, started to sweat a little, that she had found all this out. Considering the situation I wasn't too worried about it just a little nervous. And there was a huge part of me that wanted to tell her with her hearing it for the first time. But again she never said a work or alluded to anything else. Later that afternoon I was given permission to take a short walk around the hospital wing, Carrie holding my hand the entire time. I was still very stiff and my chest felt heavy and tight from smoke inhalation but I could breathe easier when I stood up. The burns on my legs had started itching as they healed and the stitches on my arms and back pulled slightly when I moved but overall I felt okay. We made our way to Bryce's room.

Bryce was still laid up in bed, the TV blaring loudly in his room, but he looked none the worse for wear. Like me he had a few burns and some minor cuts and scrapes; mostly they were treating him for smoke inhalation as well. He grinned when we entered. "Hey guys, how are you?" Bryce asked, catching me in a one-armed hug and kissing Carrie on the cheek when we came up to the bed. "I feel like I'm eighty with allergies but I can't complain." I replied with a smile. "And you?"

"Oh I'm fine, just inhaled a lot of smoke is all," he told me with a shrug. He sobered up and looked at me seriously. I tried to go back in for you and the kid, but the house began to crumble and I just couldn't get back in. I really thought you were dead when I couldn't find you and, then the firefighters wouldn't let me near the house no matter how much I fought them. They finally told me they were taking you to the hospital but they still wouldn't tell me if you were okay or not. Man, I hated not knowing."

He looked me over once more. "So you're really okay?"

I nodded. "I'm a little stiff and sore, but nothing dire. You feel okay to walk?"

"Walk where?"

"We're going to meet Allen," I said.

Bryce grinned but Carrie looked confused. "Allen?, Who's Allen?"

When she looked at me she suddenly seemed to understand. "That's the little boy's name? Allen?" She sat down with tears in her eyes. "Just like Peyton's-?" she started to say but broke off to cover her mouth with her hand.

Bryce smiled and repeated the name under his breath as well. We were all thinking the same thing.

"His mother, Olivia, came to see me last night," I told them both. "We spoke for a little while and I asked if it would be okay if we met her son and she said yes. I figured we could go check in on him and see if he's awake and up for visitors."

Bryce grinned. "That's a great idea." "Uh, maybe I should change first," he said, motioning to his thin hospital gown.

We waited for Bryce to get up and moving and then strolled down the hall to Allen's room. The sign at the door said 2B and inside on the bed was a small, frail boy with wild, bushy hair. Olivia sat next to him, holding his hand, and there was a soft *whoosh* as the machine next to his bed helped him breathe.

Olivia saw us walk up and smiled, motioning for us to come into the room. We walked in quietly and took up the space around the bed.

"How is he?" I asked.

"He's going to be fine," Olivia told us with a bright grin, glancing back at her sleeping son "They want to keep him for a few more days because he inhaled so much smoke but otherwise he's totally fine." She hugged Bryce and then turned to Carrie. "Is this your wife?" she asked me.

"Yes it is," I said, slipping an arm around Carrie's shoulders. "Carrie, I would like you to meet Olivia Banks."

Olivia reached out to shake Carrie's hand but ended up pulling her into a hug as well. "It's so nice to meet you, Carrie. I can't tell you how grateful I am to your husband and all he did. We wouldn't be here if it wasn't for these two." Both Bryce and I flushed from the compliments and then Bryce cleared his throat softly. "We wanted to stop by and see if we could meet Allen but we don't want to wake him-"

"No, no, it's fine, he hasn't been asleep long. Besides, I want him to meet the men who saved us." She leaned over and laid a hand on Allen's shoulder, speaking quietly. "Allen?, Allen, sweetie wake up."

A few seconds later his eyes fluttered open and he smiled up at his mom. She helped him sit up and he pulled the oxygen mask away from his face.

"There's some people here to meet you, honey," his mother told him and he seemed to realize for the first time we were standing there.

"This is Jeff and his brother Bryce," Olivia continued, nodding to us. "They're the ones who saved us."

"Hi," Allen said, waving weakly through a coughing fit.

I walked closer to him and stuck my hand out for him to shake it. "It's a pleasure to meet you, Allen." All of a sudden I was fighting not to cry; it was impossible to not see Peyton when I looked at him laying there.

He shook my hand and smiled. "It's nice to meet you too, sir."

Bryce stepped forward to shake his hand as well and Allen looked between us curiously. "Are you guys firefighters?"

"No," I answered., "Just was in the right place at the right time and you looked like you could use a hand."

He smiled real big and coughed again. "I don't know how to thank you guys."

"Well, there is one thing you could do," Bryce said with a smile. "What's that?" Allen asked.

"You could let us take you fishing when you get out of here. That is if it's okay with your mom, of course," he said, winking at Olivia who was on the verge of tears again. She nodded and sniffled and Carrie rubbed her back comfortingly.

Allen grinned and nodded. "Okay, but I'm pretty good at fishing. Hope you don't mind getting out-fished."

We all laughed, enjoying the lightness of the moment and just the miracle that brought us all together. But after a few minutes Allen's eyes began to droop and it was clear he needed more rest so we showed ourselves to the door. Carrie paused to give Olivia our number before we left and told her to call us if she needed anything.

We were almost into the hallway when we heard Allen's soft voice call out, "bye guys, you're my heroes!"

He sounded so much like Peyton then that I felt my breath catch in my throat. I didn't care about being a hero, I didn't care that my back itched or that my whole body ached or anything else. All I could hear in my head was Allen (and Peyton's) voice saying *'you're my hero!'*

It's what Peyton used to say every night before he went to bed and it's all I thought about for the rest of the day.

Chapter 14

The next day both Bryce and I were released from the hospital and told to go home and take it easy for a few more days while we recovered. Which was fine with me because I fell asleep the minute we got home and didn't wake up again until sometime the next morning.

I woke up to the sound of murmuring outside, like a muffled rock concert was taking place outside our bedroom window. I peeked outside and saw several news vans and reporters hanging around in the driveway, waiting for a chance to speak with us.

Carrie walked in a few minutes later, two coffee mugs in her hands, and handed me one. "They've been here all morning," she told me, looking out the window as well. "I think they want to hear your story."

I smiled at Carrie and shook my head. "They'll leave soon enough. I"ll give a couple statements and they'll scurry off to write their stories."

"Guess you should put some clothes on, then," Carrie said, smirking at my boxers and robe.

I smiled back and looked back out the window, drinking my coffee and watching the reporters mill around in our driveway. I couldn't help but to think of Willis Riley and how I would love to rub this in his face, but I also didn't want to see him either. One encounter with that man was enough to last the rest of my life.

I knew I would eventually have to face the crowd outside so I got dressed slowly, mindful of my still healing injuries, and made my way into the living room. Carrie was waiting for me and squeezed my hand as we both walked up to the door. We took a deep breath to steady ourselves and opened the door to the chaos. The reporters all rushed forward at once, speaking all together in a garbled drone, and stopped right at the foot of the steps leading up to the porch. I looked out at them, feeling a flash of irritation at their intrusion into our lives, and started speaking. "Okay, listen, I'm only going to answer a few questions here so if you want answers then stop screaming and ask one at a time so I'm not having to repeat myself."

"Mr Lockler, is it true you didn't know the family you pulled to safety?" A pretty young brunette woman with long hair asked.

"Yes, we've never met them before. My brother and I just happened to be in the area and did what anyone else would have done."

"Were you injured at all?" A reporter standing behind her asked.

"A few cuts and scrapes and some superficial burns but nothing major. The boy and his mother are safe as well, they're recovering at the hospital." I answered and remembered the reporters from earlier, I thought I hated them at the time, but these people didn't seem too bad. I never answered a single question from the last inquiry on Riley's story. That's probably why they went away so fast. This time I didn't really mind answering the questions, it felt more understood I guess, it felt more right.

"Do you plan on having any continued contact with the family?, I mean you did save their lives?"

"I sure hope so. I would love to keep contact with them but more importantly I'm just glad they're both okay."

"What do you have to say about Willis Riley and his story about you?" A tall, bald headed man asked from way in the back.

Carrie cut her eyes at me and grabbed my hand. I think she knew something had happened that was not explainable, but this was proof. But she remained stoic and stood and listened to my answer

"I think Willis Riley's story was very hurtful and not an accurate reflection of what really happened. He took a very raw, painful tragedy and exploited it for personal gain. Yes, it's true that I developed a drinking problem after my son's death but he had no right to share that information with the public. As for the rest, Mr. Riley took a very personal experience and spun it to make us appear crazy and delusional. What my brother and I experienced was real, that's all I'll say about it, and nothing Willis Riley says or does will change that."

"Do you consider yourself a hero, Mr. Lockler?" The pretty woman from earlier asked.

I smiled and shook my head. "No ma'am. Like I said, Bryce and I just happened to be in the right place at the right time and we did exactly what anyone else would have done when they saw someone in trouble. I just did what I know my son would've done. Thank you, that's all!"

I looked back at Carrie and ushered her back inside, the buzz of yelling of questions fading behind us as we closed the door.

"Carrie honey, come sit down, I wanna tell you what happened finally!"

The look in her eyes was of shear exhaustion, but I could tell she desperately wanted to know, so she quickly came and sat in the chair I pulled from the dining room table.

"Ok, I'm going to tell you the story, but please don't ask questions until the end. I want you to just listen and let me get it out. And before I say anything, please understand that Bryce and I didn't tell you this only because I wanted to do this on my own and I think Bryce was meant to be there. And most importantly, I didn't want to add more pressure to you, so please don't be mad."

"Jeff, I couldn't be mad at you, no matter what you say. A very good thing came out of whatever happened, and I think a very much improved, great man came out of this. I promise that this is a good thing, and I think you and I will be fine, so tell me the story, and I will not be mad!" She said that holding my hand and kissing me as I knelt down before her.

"Ok" I said "here it goes, I went to get bourbon at the liquor store, I was very drunk and very hungover, I have no recollection of how it happened but I ended up at The Cover and right were Peyton had died. I stood there crying and then I heard Peyton talk to me. He gave me a message, and I came home like a bat out of hell and Bryce called as soon as I walked in the house, so I told him about it and the next day we went out there.

Peyton kept giving us messages and they were a day, a time, and an address! So we showed up when and where Peyton told us to be and we found the house on fire. That's why we were there honey, and it was a true miracle! I don't know how it's explained, but it is what happened, do you believe me?"

Carrie exploded up out of the chair kicking it backwards across the kitchen, she hugged me as hard as she could. She was crying but through the tears she said "I knew it, I knew something magical had happened, I felt it before it even took place. I love you!"

She pulled her head back and kissed me deeply, and said "you don't have to say anymore, or ever speak of it again, because I believe you and its impossible to be mad. I believe that things happen for a reason, or that a chain of events has to work in the correct order, the stars have to align, whatever you want to call it! And that's why life is so hard, and so challenging, but yet so fun."

I don't really, truly, know how she never found out. I think about it and it sounds absurd that she never found out before I told her. With the news and the reporters, I know they went away pretty fast but still you would think she would've found out somehow someway. I mean it's possible that she did know and just didn't convey anything to me. And you know what, if she did and just didn't tell me, I didn't care. She not one time mentioned it again, nor did I.

Chapter 15

It was still early in the morning but I didn't protest when Carrie asked if I wanted to go back to the bedroom, a playful glint in her eye. I let her lead me back down the hallway, flipping the blinds as we walked to block out the reporters still lingering outside. A little while later we were laying in bed together, arms wrapped around each other, and I happened to glance out the window to the trees standing tall outside our house. High up in the treetops, almost invisible from my limited view in the bedroom, I saw a massive eagle perched on a branch. It sat there motionless, its broad chest puffed out, and then turned its head toward the house. It seems strange but I swear it was looking directly at me.

I felt goosebumps prickle along my arms; it was like I was looking right at God, and he was looking right back at me.

After a few weeks everything had somewhat returned to normal and Carrie and I were slowly getting back to our regular lives. At least until someone knocked on our door one evening.

I opened it to find Olivia and Allen standing on the front porch. They both looked disheveled and cold, shivering under the glow of the porch light.

"What's going on?" I asked, noticing the tears in Olivia's eyes. She shook her head, clearly upset, and Carrie stepped out to pull her inside. "Come inside, both of you, and tell us what's going on." Olivia and Allen allowed themselves to be pulled inside and I closed the door behind them. After a second, Olivia had composed herself enough to speak. "The insurance company called today., Apparently the policy won't cover much and they said they probably won't be able to rebuild my house. We don't have any money and nowhere else to go and-" she stopped, choking back a sob.

The house that Oivia and Allen were living in was owned by her ex husband, that's why the name on the mailbox read 'The Wileys" He had taken off about two years before all this happened leaving her and her son behind. She took odd jobs and dated from time to time, she wasn't skilled at too much. She was raised in a household that the woman did the housework and the men brought home the money. So when it came to job skills she didn't have much to fall back on. They were not in a good situation at all, financially and little Allen needed a father figure as well, but then the fire was just too much.

Carrie and I shared a look before she pulled Olivia into her arms and rubbed her back soothingly. "Honey, don't worry about that right now. I'll talk to some of the members of our church and see if they can help out. Until then you and Allen can stay here with us."

Olivia's eyes widened and she shook her head adamantly. "Oh, no, no, no, we can't impose on you guys like that. I just needed someone to talk to and-" Carrie just shook her head. "Olivia, sweetie, it's not up for discussion. You are staying here until we can get you guys settled into a new place and that's final."

In the meantime, Allen had wandered into the living room and settled on the couch, curling up against the cushions and watching whatever was playing on the TV. I grinned and nodded toward him. "See, Allen doesn't mind making himself at home." Olivia still seemed hesitant. "Guys, we can't just barge in on you like this. I mean we don't have anything, no clothes, no money, no-" Carrie just shook her head again. "Don't worry about that now. Jeff and I have plenty of space here and first thing tomorrow I'm taking you and Allen shopping to get some new clothes. Now, there's a bathroom down the hall here. Why don't you go take a hot shower and get warmed up and when you get out we'll sit down and have dinner together and figure out sleeping arrangements."

Olivia finally relented, tearfully thanking us over and over, before taking Carrie's advice and wandering down the hall toward the bathroom. Carrie went to the kitchen to get dinner started so I went into the living room to check in on Allen. He was still curled up on the couch and watching the TV with the kind of blank detachment that comes from being completely exhausted. He looked like he was barely awake when I walked into the room and gave me a sleepy half-smile when I sat down on the couch beside him. I had no idea what he was watching but when I glanced at the screen I felt my heart skip a beat. There on the screen was The Wizard of Oz. I remembered one of my last conversations with Peyton, about his musings about where the mythical land of Oz was located, and it felt strangely appropriate that Allen was watching the same movie now.

I sat there with Allen for a while until it became apparent I was the only one watching the movie anymore; Allen was fast asleep on the couch. Standing quietly, I walked out of the room and went to the garage to tinker around. We had a guest room but it was pretty sparse and could use some bookshelves so I was looking around to see if we had any spare wood I could use to cobble some together. Keeping those projects in mind, I walked back inside to help Carrie finish making dinner.

The next morning Carrie took Olivia and Allen to go shopping while I stayed home and got the guest room set up. It wasn't much but it would be comfortable enough while they stayed with us. Bryce stopped by around noon to help me rearrange the furniture and make sure the room was as comfortable as we could make it.

Later that afternoon, Carrie, Olivia, and Allen got back home and judging from the bags around their wrists, it was clear the shopping trip had been successful. Olivia took Allen into the guest bedroom so they could put away their new clothes and Carrie came into the kitchen with me to start dinner.

It had been a long time since I flexed my culinary skills in the kitchen and I forgot how much I enjoyed cooking. I made meatloaf filled with onions and peppers and mashed potatoes on the side. The kitchen smelled heavenly and I realized for the first time I hadn't eaten all day.

When the meatloaf was done, we called Olivia and Allen into the kitchen and sat down for dinner. We said Grace, another thing I hadn't done in a long time since Peyton died, and dug in. We had just started eating when I looked over and noticed both Olivia and Allen eating ravenously like they hadn't had a good, hearty meal in weeks. The thought broke my heart.

Olivia noticed and stopped, glancing at me sheepishly. "What's wrong?"

I realized I had been staring and shook my head. "Oh nothing, I just didn't realize how good my meatloaf was," I joked, earning a small smile from both Olivia and Allen. It was a quick recovery but; I didn't want to allude to the real issue.

"So Olivia," I began, poking at my mashed potatoes with my fork. "We have you set up in the guest room but I was wondering, what would you think about letting me turn the garage into a mini apartment for Allen? That'll give both of you a little more room and it will be more comfortable for you both. Also, I think we could sneak a TV in there for him," I said, winking as Allen beamed at me.

From the corner of my eye I caught Carrie giving me a strange look. I wasn't sure what it was for but kept talking anyway. "It won't take long at all to get it all fixed up."

Olivia chimed in at that moment. "Jeff, please don't go out of your way, it's plenty fine what you guys have done already, trust me. Allen and I can stay in the that guest room until we get back on our feet."

"Oh, trust me, it's no trouble at all. With Bryce's carpentry skills we could get a really sweet room set up for him."

Carrie was still watching me with that strange look on her face but I still wasn't sure what it meant and I didn't want to ask in front of Olivia and Allen. There was very little conversation after that as we finished up the meal.

When dinner was over Olivia stood to help clean up the kitchen and Allen disappeared off into the living room again. Bryce grabbed a beer and walked out to the garage to survey the work that I so eloquently put on him without asking. Once the dishes were all put away, Olivia walked into the living room and sat down next to Allen, the boy snuggling up to her almost immediately. It reminded me of Peyton and I felt a small smile tug at my lips. I was just about to turn and walk into the garage to help Bryce when Carrie caught me by the arm. "Can we talk outside?" she asked quietly, her expression somber.

I nodded and followed her outside, closing the door behind me. "Jeff, sweetheart, I'm glad you want to take care of Olivia and Allen, I do too, but don't you think it would be easier to let Allen have Peyton's-"

"Peyton's what?" I asked, cutting her off before she has a chance to finish.

"Well, Peyton's room, of course," Carrie said as if it was the most obvious answer in the world.

I shook my head. "No, the garage will be a lot better for him. We'll get it all fixed up and he'll have plenty of space to play and some privacy too and-"

"Jeff," Carrie started again, her voice gentle. "Honey, do you think the reason you're so hesitant to give up Peyton's room is because you still can't bring yourself to go in there?"

I knew it was coming, I knew it, yet I didn't anticipate how I would feel and react.

She continued, "Sweetheart, with all that we've gone through and with everything that's happened don't you think it's time to start facing this head on? Peyton would want Allen to have his room, Jeff. He would be so proud of everything you're doing for this family and how much you've helped them. I know this is a difficult decision but maybe it's time to break past that last barrier so we can move forward." it's been super hard for you, and me as well. But Jeff it's time that you break that last barrier and finally move forward."

I shook my head, suddenly irritated at the very idea of giving up Peyton's room. "No, we're leaving his room as is. It's all we have left of him, Carrie, I'm not giving that up. I'm sorry, I just can't."

Carrie sat down and looked at me with tears in her eyes. "We have more left of Peyton left than just his room, Jeff. Why can't you see that?"

I didn't have an answer for her so I just walked back inside and left the questions unanswered. How dare her, I did everything Peyton asked me to do and that should be good enough.

Chapter 16

I wasn't sure why Carrie's suggestion of letting Allen have Peyton's room bothered me so much but I stewed about it for the rest of the night. I couldn't stand to speak to anyone else, not then, so I made my way down the hall to the bedroom and decided to just call it a night.

I changed clothes and got into bed and stared up at the ceiling as the irritation continued gnawing at me. How could she suggest such a thing? Yes, I was happy Olivia and Allen were staying with us but how could she suggest giving up our son's room like that? What was I supposed to say? Sure, go ahead and move into my dead son's room. Here, play with all his toys and use all his stuff and let's all pretend everything is fine and he wasn't killed in a freak accident two years ago.

I wasn't letting that room go, I decided stubbornly; it was going to stay exactly how it is. Maybe Carrie was right and Peyton would want me to let it go and give it to Allen, maybe I hadn't completely moved on, but I didn't care. I wasn't backing down or caving at all.

I'm not sure when I eventually fell asleep but the next time I opened my eyes the sun was just rising. Carrie had slipped in at some point and was still sleeping peacefully and in spite of my irritation the night before, I got dressed quietly and stepped out of the room to let her sleep.

I planned to work in the garage that day so I slipped on my work boots and headed out into the living room. Not surprisingly, Allen was up and flipping through the channels on the TV, flashing me a bright, toothy grin when I walked in. As irritated as I had been with the idea of giving him Peyton's room I couldn't be mad at Allen."Hey buddy, you want to help me in the garage today? We'll get your bachelor pad all set up." That seemed to pique his interest and he slid off the couch to follow me into the garage. Bryce had done a couple quick sketches the night before of what could be done in the garage so it would help to get Allen's opinion on things, especially if it was going to be his room.

Without Bryce there wasn't much we could do other than plan so I took the time to teach Allen a few basic measuring techniques and how to read the diagrams Bryce had left behind. Allen was a smart kid and very fast learner and after a little while it almost seemed like he knew more about this stuff than I did. Granted, we were both novices compared to Bryce; this was his area of expertise.

The man in question appeared a few hours later, closer to noon, and joined us in the garage. Wanting to keep little hands and feet out of the way of large, heavy tools, I sent Allen inside to check in with his mom.

"What's up, buddy?" I greeted Bryce after Allen disappeared back into the house."Oh not much, just coming to make sure you hadn't started building the Taj Mahal without me," he teased, taking another look around the garage.

He was avoiding my eyes and I knew then something was bothering him. I didn't say anything, walking around and helping him finalize measurements in the garage. Another hour went by of us barely speaking before it finally got so awkward I had to say something.

"Alright, what is it?"

"What?"

"Dude you haven't said but like two words to me since you got here. What's the deal?"

He sighed heavily and shook his head. "Jeff, I talked to Carrie last night after you stormed off. She just wanted to-"

I shook my head. "Oh trust me, I know what she was trying to say and I don't want to hear it. And I definitely don't need you getting involved when this isn't any of your business." I said interrupting him.

Jeff sighed. "Jeff, I don't want to get involved in this either but I think Carrie is right. You're not moving on, man. It's like you're trying to live stuck between the past and the present and it defeats the purpose of everything we've been through."

"Peyton's room is the last thing I have of him, Bryce, and I'm not giving that up! End of discussion!"

I shook my head in frustration. "You weren't there, Bryce, you weren't there to hear that crack of lightning or see his lifeless body laying there and know there was nothing you could do!"

Angry, frustrated tears streaked down my face. "I have lived with the guilt of his death every day for the past two years and now it seems like everyone is trying to erase him. Carrie tells me to move on, you tell me to move on, but I can't, Bryce! He was my son! I should have protected him and I couldn't! And now you both want me to give up the last piece I have of him? The last thing that wasn't taken away when he died?"

I couldn't speak anymore, I was too angry, so I spun on my heel and bolted out of the garage. I didn't want to speak to Carrie or Bryce or anyone else; I needed to get out.

I shoved my way into the house, surprising Olivia and Allen who were sitting on the couch, and grabbed my car keys. Allen called out for me but I didn't stop or turn around or acknowledge him in any way. It was raining heavily when I stepped outside, the raindrops stinging my skin with each impact, but I didn't care. I got in the car and sped out of the driveway like someone was chasing me.

I drove without a destination in mind, speeding through traffic and winding roads, my hands gripping the steering wheel in a white-knuckle grasp. The tires spun on the wet road and my car swerved dangerously, forcing me to pull off to the side of the road and stop.

I practically threw myself out of the car, landing on my knees in the mud and then took off into the trees. I didn't know where I was going and it really didn't matter, I just kept running. I was crying again, hot tears mingling with the cold rain as it streamed down my face but I didn't have it in me to wipe it away.

My foot caught on a loose rock and I tumbled to the ground, landing in a messy heap. It was only then that I looked up and finally realized where I was.

I was back at The Cover.

In spite of the rain, everything seemed new and fresh, the trees still as tall and green as they'd ever been. I gazed around like I was seeing everything for the first time, like I'd found a new land. Eventually I pulled myself up and stumbled over to the pond, trying to find my reflection in the rippling water and having no luck.

I don't know what drew me to it but I found myself walking over to the tree where Peyton was killed. The memories of that night were still fresh and raw in my mind, the sight of my son lying broken and lifeless at the base of the tree, and before I knew it I was screaming out into the tree. It was a horrible, guttural sound, one I hadn't made since that night, and it felt just as raw.

I collapsed to my knees sobbing, holding onto myself like I was going to break apart at the seams. I cried until I couldn't breathe, until every ounce of my being was reduced to nothing but tears and anguish, and then I cried some more.

I don't know how long I laid there, sobbing and shivering in the rain, before it happened, I heard Peyton.

"Dad."

I whipped my head up and looked around the clearing, hoping this was all some kind of long, horrible dream and he was about to come walking out of the trees.

"Dad."

I sniffled and tried to answer. "I'm here," I mumbled brokenly. The perfect circle up light that had reared it's beautiful shine again. It lit up The Cover through the rain and the murkiness.

"It's okay, dad." Peyton's voice seemed to bounce around in my brain, filling my thoughts and drowning out everything else. "Everything happens for a reason." Those words hit me and sunk deep, settling in my soul and filling me with a warmth I never thought I'd experience again.

The hair on the back of my neck stood up and butterflies filled my stomach; I couldn't even feel the rain anymore.

The thoughts and warm feeling flooded my body and I just looked through The Cover with a smile. I finally felt at peace with everything that had happened and understood what Bryce and Carrie were talking about, what I had seemed to miss the whole time.

This was a plan of someone I could even fathom.

I knew what I had to do and what Peyton was asking of me. He always was wise beyond his years. "Thank you, son," I whispered, sniffling as I looked out over the trees. The light shot up through the trees and dissipated. I smiled once more, turned, and made my way back to the car.

The rain had slowed nearly to a stop by the time I got back home and the sun was trying to peek through the clouds overhead. With any luck it would all blow over by the end of the day.

Allen and Olivia were still sitting on the couch when I walked back in and they seemed surprised to see me in my wet, disheveled state. Carrie was sitting at the kitchen table, Bryce across from her, and they both gave me the same surprised look.

"Jeff, honey, where have you been? You've been gone for hours," Carried said, standing and walking over to me.

I caught her by the hands and pressed a kiss to her palm. "Everyone" I announced, looking around the room. "There's something I need to say."

I took a breath before beginning. "First of all, I want to apologize for my behavior earlier. That was uncalled for and I'm truly sorry for my outburst. Second, I had an epiphany when I was driving that I want to share with you all."

"What's a pafeny, Mr. Jeff?" Allen asked, eliciting a chuckle from his mother at the mispronunciation.

"It means I came to a conclusion, buddy. I realize I've been quite selfish up until now and without this epiphany I don't know that I would have been able to see that. And after I take a quick shower I will tell you." I scurried to the shower and hosed off, through on my pajamas a hurried back into the living room.

Carrie seemed to know what was about to happen and covered her mouth with her hand, tears shining in her eyes.

I reached out my hand to Allen. "Allen, come here, buddy, there's something I want to show you."

The little boy hopped up and ran to my side, taking my hand in his own. I walked slowly down the hallway toward Peyton's room, Olivia following curiously behind us.

"Okay Allen, what I'm about to show you is simple; it's nothing great or fancy but it's very important to me and I hope it will be important to you as well." I let go of his hand and motioned to Peyton's room. "Allen, this was my son's room. I want you to have it and treat it like it's yours."

Allen stopped for a second and then asked "Mr. Jeff, will your son not need it anymore?"

The lump hit my throat but I managed to smile past it. "No, buddy, he won't. But that doesn't mean you can't have it."

"So it's ok if I have his room and sleep in there and play, Mr. Jeff?" Allen asked, staring at the closed door.

"Yes," I told him, placing my hand on the top of his head. "It's all yours, everything in here you can have." I had thought it would be a lot harder to do this, to give up something so personal, but it felt right.

I opened the door and looked inside for the first time since Peyton died. That lump crept back up in my throat as I peered around at his room, smiling at how messy it was. Some of his toys laid strewn around his bed, which wasn't made, and his toy chest was still open.

Allen walked in behind me and looked around, carefully picking up a few of Peyton's old toys and turning them in his hands. He walked over to the bed and sat down, playing with the toy in his hands and admiring his new room. I stood there and watched Allen play for a minute and then slowly made my way in.

The room still smelled like Peyton. I couldn't describe it exactly but I knew I'd remember that smell for the rest of my life. I turned on the ceiling fan, the breeze stirred up dust that was spinning around. Carrie and I hadn't touched his room since he perished. Carrie would look into it, but she never cleaned it or moved anything around.

I wandered into the garage and found an old TV tucked away in one corner, a VHS copy of the Wizard of OZ still stuck in the VCR. A small smile tugged at the corner of my mouth.

He was still sitting on the bed when I walked back in and got the TV set up, pressing play so the movie would start. Olivia was in there sitting on the bed with him, she kissed him goodnight and made her way to her new room for the night. When he realized what movie it was, Allen beamed at me and jumped off the bed, running over to me and throwing his arms around my waist.

"You're my hero, Mr. Jeff," he said, hugging me as hard as he could.

It was all I could do not to tear up at that. Instead I hugged him back, ruffling his hair gently the same way I used to do with Peyton. I walked him back over to the bed and helped him get settled in for the night. Just before I turned off the light, I looked back and swore for just a moment I saw Peyton laying there. I smiled and closed the door. My knees buckled and I almost fell to the floor. I had remained calm and stoic and surprisingly held back the tears. That was no more, I wept like I hadn't wept in a while. It wasn't a bellow or a scream but a nice controlled sob. I felt the weight lift from my shoulders my heart beat like a drum and sweat pooled in my clinched fists, I crouched there in front of Allen's new room and felt weightless for a second. I was overcome with emotions yet some how felt serene, like it was final, complete.

Carrie was waiting for me in the hall and she pulled me into her arms. "I'm so proud of you, baby," she whispered to me, pressing a kiss to my temple.

I hugged her back tightly. "You're my angel, Carrie," I whispered back.

I caught sight of Bryce making his way to the door and walked over to stop him. "Man, look, I am so sorry about earlier, I didn't mean-"

Bryce waved a hand to cut me off. "Water under the bridge, brother," he said with a grin. "I figured you needed to just blow off some steam and I knew a visit to The Cover would do the trick."

I frowned in confusion. "How did you know I went back to The Cover?"

Bryce just shrugged. "Call it a feeling," he said with a knowing smile. "Miraculous things happen out there so I figured that's where you were heading when you left earlier."

He smiled again and patted me on the shoulder before turning and walking out to his car. I waved as he pulled away and reached over to pull Carrie into my arms. "This was part of the plan the whole time," I said, pressing a kiss to Carrie's forehead and walking back inside.

So that's the story, and what a wild one it is I must say. The thing is I learned so much during all this and one thing stuck with me and this will forever remain in my heart. And it's that I'm not claiming to know the secret of life but what I do know is that nothing under the sun will last forever. So knowing that, we should cherish each other and take nothing for granted.

Take what you have and embrace it with everything you can give. Tell your loved ones how much you love them, and hug them as much as you can. I'm glad I learned that lesson even if it took me a while to get there. Regardless of what happens in life, just remember, we are all one, under the sun!

I walked inside to start this new life of mine.

THE END

This book is dedicated to the men and women that have fought and continue to fight for our freedom! And to my family and friends, you know who you are. Thanks for the love and support, I love you all!

Jason M. Freeman

Printed in the United States
By Bookmasters